A WESLEY CLUB MYSTERY ADVENTURE

Montana's Mission: Protecting the Forest

VICTOR HESS

Book Cover and Formatting provided by Trisha Fuentes

ISBN: 978-0999564066

To those who protect the forest

CHAPTER 1

Sunday, May 11, 1958, 2 a.m.
Glen Helen Nature Preserve, Yellow Springs, Ohio

Vince and Max Arledge tramped their way down Stepping Stone Trail to Talus Trail in Glen Helen. It was just one of the many footpaths meandering fifteen miles over streams, around boulders, beside springs, up and back down steep slopes. The trails wove through a thousand acres of nature, untouched except for the paths and footbridges strategically placed to give the visitors a close awareness of God's creation. But now, it was 2 a.m. and the two intruders were not looking for a photo. Their flashlights sent beams of light through the forest, illuminating the eyes of an occasional animal until they arrived at a pair of trees at the turn of the trail.

"This is it," said Vince. "Give me those climbers."

Vince was the elder and smarter of the two brothers and clearly in charge. He looked older with his beard, but he was much shorter, by a full foot, than his younger brother.

Max handed him a pair of old rusted spikes lumber jacks used to climb trees or linemen used to climb telephone poles. He held the flashlight as Vince sat on a log and strapped the antique devices to each leg.

When Vince stood up and walked toward the tree, the spikes sounded like cowboy spurs with every step he took.

"Give me that net," Vince said. Max draped the fishing net across Vince's back. Max was tall and lanky. His face was narrow, and his eyes set deep in his skull, giving him a creepiness noticed by most people who met him.

"Now, the rope." Max gave him the 50' coil of sisal rope they had purchased earlier that day at the hardware store.

As he draped the rope on Vince's shoulder, Max felt something move near his leg and side stepped in such a way that he lost his balance, falling backwards into Yellow Springs Creek, totally soaking his pants. The splash caused a commotion among some of the birds and nighttime animals.

"Shh," said Vince, irritated. "What are you doing?"

"Something touched me. Does this place have snakes?" Max reached for the limb of a small tree and pulled himself upright.

"This place has everything." There was a loud smack in the water and Max leaped out of the creek, his hand grabbing at the coil of rope draped over Vince's shoulder nearly pulling him over.

"Stop it," whispered Vince.

"Seriously, what was that?" Max asked.

"Probably an otter or something. They live here, you idiot." They stood there for a moment looking around, making sure they were still alone. The rushing sound of a nearby spring, the whistling of a screech owl, and the soft breeze soothed their anxiety.

"Are you okay?" Vince finally asked.

"My shoes are soaked. My pants are wet and falling off."

"Well, I'm ready. You'll just have to tighten your belt," said Vince, who had taken on the silhouette of a mountain climber against the bright half-moon.

"Are you sure this is the right tree? It isn't very big around," he said while hitching up his pants.

"The nest is in that tree." He pointed to a large oak just next to the pine. "It's too wide to climb with just these climbers. But this pine goes all the way up right next to the nest in the oak tree." Max looked straight up the tall pine and nearly fell backward the more he stared.

"What if they ain't there? Don't they feed at night?" Max said while he adjusted his neck.

"It's May. There should be an egg or two up there. If there is, the mother or father will be sitting on it." Vince started climbing up the tall pine. The spike from the climber didn't catch on the first try and his right foot skidded down the trunk.

"Ouch!" yelled Vince.

"Shh." Max pulled on Vince's arm.

"What?"

"I saw something. Over there." Max pointed toward the light of the moon. "It's a bear."

"There ain't no bears here. Let go. I've got this." Vince grasped the tree trunk, and this time firmly planted his climber spike in the soft pine wood. He slowly straightened his leg and rose a foot above Max. He repeated it with the other leg, raising himself another foot, and again until he was well above Max. Max backed away from the tree and watched his older brother disappear into the pine limbs until he could no longer hear the clank of the climbers.

Suddenly, Max heard a ruckus up in the pine tree, just where it met the eagle's nest. The moonlight illuminated tiny feathers floating, pine limbs falling, and then there were screeches from the eagles, and finally, the scream from Vince.

Max stepped back a step and stared back up into the pine limbs, heart racing but unable to see Vince. He heard a continuous cracking of the wood and finally watched pine limbs slowly fall toward him and then Vince's frantic face appeared closer and closer until it all fell directly on Max, forcing him back into the creek under the fallen pine tree. Now Vince lay on the top side of the tree, his mouth full of feathers, the net torn to shreds.

"Did you get the eagle?" Max said.

"I had him. How come the tree fell?" Vince yelled. "What did you do?"

There was a scurrying along the creek and then a screech from the oak, which was still standing, but the entire pine tree was laying across the creek.

Whoosh. The eagle appeared and swooped down directly toward the brothers. Vince raised his arm to protect his face but then the eagle glided by and plucked a squirrel from the fallen pine tree and with just a few strokes of his wings ascended back to his nest. The squirrel barked a protest and then became silent.

Vince and Max crawled from the limbs of the pine tree. Vince, rope still wrapped around his shoulder, limped around the tree.

"Didn't you see this?" he yelled at Max.

"What?"

"This." He pointed at the base of the pine, chipped away neatly like it was a yellow pencil sharpened with a pen knife. A loud slap on the water made them both jump.

"Beaver!" Vince said. "How did I miss this?" There was another loud slap on the water.

"Hey! What's going on down there. Who's there?" A voice came from the top of the 100 limestone steps leading down to the Glen.

"The Baron is not going to be happy," said Max.

"Stop right there!" the man yelled.

"Let's get out of here. Follow me," said Vince, and he led Max up the Stepping Stone Trail toward where they parked the car on the far side of the Glen. A beam of light swept the forest below the Trailside Museum, quiet again except for the fading sound of two men running and tripping up the trail.

CHAPTER 2

Sunday, May 11, 1958, Noon
John Bryan Park Mother's Day Picnic

Nearly 100 people showed up to the Trinity Methodist Church Mother's Day Picnic at John Bryan State Park in Yellow Springs, Ohio. John Bryan State Park is the picnic and camping area adjacent to Glen Helen and Clifton Gorge. Abundant trails pass from one park to the other and despite the marked trails it's easy to get lost in the huge, wooded area. Combined, there were 2,000 acres and if you added the Boy Scout Camp adjacent to the park, there would be 500 more acres. The residents of the small village of Yellow Springs were like informal caretakers of the park areas and of like-mind when it came to protecting animals and the environment. Any threat to the ecological health of the forest was justification for an organized community response.

The Mother's Day picnic was extra special because today fourteen 12- and 13-year-olds were confirmed as members of the church, an annual tradition. Today was even more special because many were also celebrating the release of Florence Williams' parents from prison after four years of being incarcerated for a crime they did not commit.

Mr. Sloan and Mr. Pyle, two of the dads, were stationed at one grill making hamburgers while two other volunteers were grilling hot dogs and sausages. Even more church members were showing up with baked beans, potato salad, and desserts. The confirmands were playing in a big circle floating two Frisbees back and forth when Sally Sloan pointed to the edge of the woods.

"Look," she whispered. All eyes turned to a doe and two fawns just within the tree line. The doe's ears twitched. Montana MacCarthy, one of the confirmands, dropped the Frisbee she was holding and slowly walked toward the deer. Her red hair fell straight down her back in stark contrast to the white shirt she and the other confirmands were wearing that day. She looked back at the kids and brought her finger to her lips. They remained quiet and still. She and the doe locked eyes. The doe stood still, raised her head, looked around and allowed Montana to advance toward her. Finally, at about a five-foot distance, Montana stopped, and the fawns took a step toward her. What seemed like minutes was just a few seconds when Montana waved her arms, a gesture to direct the deer's retreat back into the forest. Then she came back to the circle of kids who had suddenly lost interest in Frisbee and wanted to know how she could get so close.

"She's a Dr. Doolittle," said Jesse Hall. "She can pick up birds, or pretty much anything. They love her."

This once, Montana didn't mind Jesse's comment. Even though it violated one of the Wesley Club's rules about maintaining secrecy. The Wesley Club consisted of just six kids of the confirmation class, each with a unique God-given talent and bound together to follow John Wesley's three simple rules:

First, do no harm.

Second, do all the good you can; and

Third, do all you can to be close to God.

Already, this little club solved the mystery of Florence Williams' parents being falsely imprisoned for robbery by discovering the evidence that proved their innocence. During the four years her parents were imprisoned, Florence was moved around from house to house until her Aunt Audrey rescued her from an abusive foster home with the help of Mr. Gregory, a lawyer and her boss. During her ordeal, Florence became aware of her ability to discern good and evil from auras or 'glows' as she called them, which emanated around people at various times. Montana talked to the animals and Florence could discern the good and bad in people.

"Let's eat," yelled Pastor Armey and he motioned all toward the picnic table heaped with food. He held his hands out and the group got quiet.

"Dear God, thank you for this beautiful day. Thank you for the women here, some mothers, some aunts, some sisters, some daughters, all with abundant love for the children of this world. Thank you, God, for these fourteen confirmands, who are the future of our church. May they remember all that was taught during the past few months. Thank you now for this wonderful food and the hands that prepared it. Amen."

"Amen," the group responded.

The Wesley Club sat at one picnic table with Montana and her grandparents.

As they ate, Mr. MacCarthy asked Sally, "What's that?"

Sally showed him the sketch she was working on in between bites.

"Montana walked up to these deer. It was so special," Sally said.

"Sally draws animals," said Florence. "It's her gift."

The sketch was, in every detail, exactly how the doe looked just before Montana shooed the deer away.

"Hmm," said Mr. MacCarthy.

"She does faces," said William Groves.

"From memory, too," said Dale, eager to join in.

"You might be just what we're looking for. I run the Trailside Museum in Glen Helen and we want to put together a wildlife pamphlet. This is an amazing likeness. Have you ever done birds?"

Sally turned back a few pages in her sketch book. "Here's a robin I did yesterday at our house." The picture showed the robin's beak working the soil between blades of grass.

"Drawings and photos. That's what we're looking for. It has to appeal to elementary kids," said Montana's grandpa.

"Janice Pyle. She's our photographer," said Sally and looked around the gathering.

"Janice, Janice, over here," she yelled once she spotted the assistant youth director taking pictures of the gathering. She turned her attention back to the sketch pad.

"How's this?" Sally said and showed him the same robin, this time winking its eye.

"Unbelievable," he said.

Florence slid close to Dale, Janice's brother, so Janice could sit at the table. In just the past two hours, Florence Williams went from a thirteen-year-old, orphaned to her aunt, back to a normal child, with her friends. Her parents, after four years in prison, sat at the next picnic table with Mr. Gregory.

Picnic Table with Mr. and Mrs. Williams

"Mr. Gregory, I don't know how this all happened. I'm afraid it will be a while before I can pay you," said Oswald Williams, as they watched Florence and the others talking with Mr. MacCarthy. One of the cooks passed out more plates of hamburgers, chips, and corn on the cob to everyone at the picnic table.

"Let me tell you what I know so far," said Mr. Gregory. "First of all, you can thank your daughter and those kids over there, because they put all the pieces together. She never stopped believing in you. The good news is you will be able to afford me because the state of West Virginia owes you a bundle for false imprisonment. We'll work on that next week. Now, if you like it here, we've got a good job waiting for you at the furniture plant. It's good pay. That's up to you. Meanwhile, you need to look for a place to live. You'll like it here."

Florence's mother, Rachel, and Florence's Aunt Audrey looked at each other with huge smiles as Florence and Montana ran over to them.

"Look, everyone." Florence pointed in the sky. "It's an eagle. Montana, there's your eagle!"

Montana stood smiling, her hand shielding her eyes. "That's her alright. She's back."

This particular eagle was feared lost for the past few days. It was one of two of Glen Helen's eagles.

Oswald looked up. "An American Bald Eagle. What a sight. Freedom."

"Look, Grandpa," yelled Montana. "It's her! She's flying! The eagle swooped close to Montana and landed on a limb just above where she was standing. "She's okay."

Then the eagle flew off before Janice could snap a picture.

Sunday, May 11, 1958, 2 p.m.
Grinnell Mill Apartment

The Arledge brothers had been recruited by Baron Reginald von Wheaton and were the prime candidates for securing him an American Bald Eagle. The eagle population was quickly dwindling, which made them very valuable around the world. The Baron was an entrepreneur, a businessman, who looked for the fast dollar, no matter whether it was legal or illegal.

Trapping, killing, or even owning an American Bald Eagle was illegal, punishable by steep fines and imprisonment of one year. A friend recommended Vince and Max Arledge, who were ten-year veteran Canadian trappers, to find him an eagle, so the Baron set them up in an apartment at the old Grinnell Mill just south of Glen Helen.

Originally, the Grinnell Mill operated as a water-powered gristmill. A large wooden waterwheel once powered the drive shaft that turned two sets of buhrstones. The mill closed in 1937 and the structure was vacant until 1948 when Antioch College bought the mill and surrounding area and incorporated it into the Glen Helen Nature Preserve. It was then that a portion of the non-operating mill was converted into an apartment where the Arledge boys now lived.

The Baron insisted on the meeting to report on the progress of finding and capturing an eagle that had been sighted in Glen Helen.

"Now, explain why there is no American Bald Eagle in that cage," said Baron von Wheaton to the Arledge brothers. "I was hoping to pay you this $500." He shuffled through the wad of twenty-dollar bills and then he put them back in the pocket of his brown leather jacket.

"You have a week to get me the bird, or you will need to find another place to stay." His German accent made the warning more intimidating.

"Don't worry, Mr. Van Wheaton, we'll get it. Seriously, I had it in my net, but the tree fell. That beaver was working on that tree for days and it decided to fall when I leaned in to get the eagle," said Vince.

"Von! Baron *von* Wheaton. How many times do I have to tell you." He glared at Vince and then cooled down. "You better have your face looked at. Did it bite you?"

"It clawed me. There are two of them and at least one egg. I think. I didn't have time to be sure." He grimaced from the pain.

"This eagle is important to me and my organization. You need this money." He pulled the wad of bills back out of his pocket and held it in front of Vince. "And I need that eagle."

The two brothers stared at the money. They were broke and this job was their stake at settling in the U. S.

"Seriously, get your face looked at," the Baron said as he opened the door to leave.

"I'll get your bird. Don't worry," said Vince. When the door shut, he looked in the mirror hanging on the wall and had not realized how much his face had swollen since last night. His forehead was scabbed up from the eagle or limbs – probably both.

"Yeah, Vince, you need to get that looked at," Max said as Vince rummaged through drawers looking for iodine or salve to ease the pain he suddenly felt.

CHAPTER 3

Monday, May 12, 1958, Noon
Central Junior High Cafeteria

Every school day, the six Wesley Club members sat at the same table in the cafeteria during lunch. At that moment all six were seated, they stopped eating, bowed their heads, and quietly said grace over the food.

"Dear God, bless this food for our nourishment and our bodies for your service. We promise to do no harm, do all the good we can, and do all we can to stay close to You. We pray this in Jesus' name, Amen."

Then they continued eating and whatever conversation they were in.

"Florence, I couldn't believe your parents got released so quickly," Sally said.

"Mr. Gregory did it. Once that other guy and his wife confessed, Mr. Gregory drove all the way to West Virginia and wouldn't leave the state without them. I thought they would be different, but it was like we never got broken up."

"Will they stay here?" asked Dale.

"That's the best part. Daddy already took a job at the furniture plant, so we're staying here. We're all staying with Aunt Audrey until Daddy finds a house. Mr. Wells is helping us."

"How's the eagle, Montana?" William asked.

"So far so good. Can you all come to the Glen after school? If we all work together, Grandpa thinks we can get the pamphlet done before school lets out for the year." She pulled out a large sheet of paper with a map of Glen Helen drawn on it. There were numbers scattered all over it. She turned it over to reveal a legend with a list of animals under each number.

"Grandpa and I worked on the list last night. If we can get twenty animals and thirty birds, he said that would be a good pamphlet. We'll show our plan to the Glen Helen Director today. Jesse, can you come?"

"I babysit today." When Jesse wasn't working at Pat's market, he'd watch his three-year-old sister while his mom worked at one of the local drug stores.

"I was hoping you could bring her."

"We can pick you up at your house," said Dale.

"We won't be there long. Please come," said Sally.

Sally and Jesse had a history beyond Xenia that went back to the third grade. They had met for just a few minutes during a time when Jesse's mom and dad divorced. At such a young age the two exchanged clover bracelets and innocently vowed to love one another. Even then, Sally had mastered her sketching skills, saving the sketch she did from the memory of then eight-year-old Jesse. However, they never saw each other again for over four years, until Sally and her parents showed up at Jesse's church in Xenia. Their feelings for each other had never changed.

"What would I do?"

"Grandpa said we need a photographer, that's Janice," said Montana. "Sally will do the sketches. Dale and William will develop the film in the darkroom, and you and Grandpa will layout the pamphlet and write the descriptions of each picture and sketch. You can do that at the Trailside Museum."

"What about Christina?"

"I might need her sometimes," Montana said.

Each of the six Wesley Club members had a gift. Montana's was communicating with animals, Sally did amazing sketches, Florence could see the good and bad in people by their glows, Jesse had his singing voice, William could memorize music and play it back on the piano, and Dale had mastered Morse Code. But it did not stop there. Jesse's three-year-old sister, Christina, could heal -- or so many in the church thought. Montana was convinced that just by holding Christina her migraine headaches would instantly stop, and for a very long time.

Jesse smiled. "Okay. I'll see you after school."

Monday, May 12, 1958, 4 p. m.
Glen Helen Trailside Museum

Mr. MacCarthy guided the Wesley Club through the small Trailside Museum.

"Is this room large enough for a darkroom? I thought it best we set it up here than over on the college campus. My photography buddies will give us what we need as far as chemicals, trays, and lights are concerned," said Mr. MacCarthy.

"This will do. Do they have a print enlarger? I'll definitely need that," said Janice Pyle.

"They promised to give us all we need. They're bringing it over tomorrow morning. They'll even set it up for you," said Mr. MacCarthy.

"Perfect. Thank you."

"Okay, then. I'll clear out this room while you kids get familiar with the area."

They all sat at the top of where 100 limestone steps led down nearly thirty feet to the bottom of the Glen. Montana held Christina in her lap, closed her eyes, and sighed with relief, immediately feeling the pain in her head ease away.

"Why doesn't the pain stay away?"

"I don't know," said Jesse. He and Sally unfolded the map of the Glen for Janice to see the plan Montana had laid out.

"The numbers in red are daytime animals. The nighttime animals we have to split up because some we can only catch early in the morning and the others around midnight. They're the blue numbers," said Montana.

"This is going to be fun," said Florence.

"It will be like a camp out. The boys will set up above Traveler's Spring. Janice and us girls will set up down there." She pointed nearly straight down to the end of the stone steps. "We'll do as much as we can with the daytime animals during the week. This weekend, Friday and Saturday, we'll see how many night animals we can get."

Tuesday May 13, 1958, 4 p. m.
Glen Helen

Montana stood six inches taller than everyone in the Wesley Club except for William, who was the same height. Montana always wore the clothes of a tomboy: jeans, flannel shirts, t-shirt underneath, and had flaming red hair. It was here that she was most at home. She loved the Glen and the animals, and they loved her.

"Grandpa said this would be a good place to sketch a beaver and raccoon. See this tree?" The girls looked at the base of the pine that had recently fallen across the creek near Talus trail.

"Look how even the cuts are. Mr. Beaver is still working on this one. These are fresh cuts where he's pulled away limbs. Probably for his dam."

Janice was intrigued by the cuts at the base of the tree and how a few limbs were cut and apparently dragged away. She took a few pictures.

"What's this?" Janice said. Her camera was aimed at the top end of the tree.

The three girls leaned over the tree studying the steel apparatus embedded in the pine wood. A leather strap was still attached but clearly torn.

"I'll ask Grandpa. We'll be here a while, so I'll get us a couple canteens."

"What's all this?" Sally asked.

"Feathers. Eagle. I'm sure." Montana looked straight up into the oak. "There it is. The eagle nest."

"It's huge," said Janice, aiming her camera directly at the massive nest of limbs, twigs, and pine needles.

"I know. Grandpa says an eagle nest can weigh a ton."

"Wow," said Sally.

"How do I get a picture of that eagle?" Janice asked.

"Don't worry, you will," Montana said, and then headed back up the steps to the Trailside Museum, where her grandpa was.

"Montana sure knows the outdoors," said Janice.

"We think she actually talks to the animals. You should see her when she gets an animal in her hands. It will look up in her face, like a puppy," said Sally.

Moments later, Montana returned with her grandfather and Florence.

"Look who I found," said Montana.

"Hey, Florence!" said Janice.

"Show me the contraption," said Mr. MacCarthy.

Montana guided them to the top end of the tree.

"That's recent. Now, why is someone climbing trees out here?"

"Look at the eagle feathers, Grandpa."

He put his hands on his hips and stared straight up the oak tree. Then he walked over to inspect the base of the fallen pine tree.

"Someone's after our eagles," he said with a look of concern.

"Do you think he was climbing it when it fell?" asked Florence.

"If he was, he's hurtin' right now," said Mr. MacCarthy. "It's against the law to use climbers to hunt."

Montana looked around and then the whole group scanned the forest.

"Look here," he said, gesturing to the dirt. "Someone fell here or jumped the creek. See this footprint?" It was a Glen Helen rule that humans stay on the trails. Only animals were allowed free run of the forest.

Janice stood very still as she took a photograph of the print. "It's a boot," she said.

"Why would someone want an eagle?" said Florence and then a glint of light got her attention for just a moment, and it was gone. It came from the cliff line up near the museum. She shielded her eyes with her hand and stared at the small shadow, moving, glowing a sinister but familiar aura that sent shivers down her spine.

"Not good guys. Someone is up there, and they glow very bad," she said. Everyone looked.

"Glow bad?" Mr. MacCarthy said.

"Grandpa," Montana said. "She has a gift. People glow good or bad. She can tell."

"A gift?"

"Yep, like me and the animals. We all have a gift."

"All of you?" he said, now looking around. "Where did you see this person or glow?"

"Up there." She stood in front of him and pointed up by the cliff line, but no one was visible now.

Tuesday May 13, 1958, 4:30 p.m.
Glen Helen Parking Lot

Vince and Max got in the 1940 Chevy Suburban.

"It's just a bunch of kids," said Vince. We'll try again tonight." Just then, a 1957 BMW Roadster pulled into the parking lot, right beside the Suburban. Baron von Wheaton quickly got in the back seat of Vince's car.

"Change of plans, boys," he said. "I spent all morning with a landscape architect to get a pond put on my farm. Do you know how much that costs? $2,200 just to move some earth and build an earth dam. Then he says he can't get to it until, get this, six months. Six months! You know what I told him?" He pulled closer to the front seat. "A beaver can build it quicker than that!" He started laughing and, of course, the Arledge boys laughed along with him.

"A beaver!" he repeated.

"Yeah, a beaver," Vince said laughing, and as hard as he could. Then the Baron stopped laughing, got very serious, leaned further forward and said, "Get me that beaver. I want that beaver."

Vince's eyes got big. "That beaver?"

"That beaver. Your beaver that knocked you guys to the ground."

"I thought you wanted an eagle?" Vince scowled.

"Get me both if you can. But I want the beaver. He's going to build me a pond." He grabbed Vince's shoulder with one hand and waved the wad of money with the other, got out of the car, slammed the door shut, and drove away in his BMW.

"How are we going to get a beaver?" asked Max.

“A trap, you idiot. Same as we did in Canada. I just need to find the plans.”

“We left all our books in Canada, didn’t we?”

“I know. We were in a hurry. Let me think.”

After three tries, he started the engine and pulled out of the museum parking lot.

CHAPTER 4

Wednesday, May 14, 1958, 10:00 a.m.
Xenia Library

The seventh-grade English class marched from the Junior High School across Edison Boulevard to the library. The Xenia Carnegie Library was built in 1906, a gift from steel baron Andrew Carnegie. A total of 2,509 Carnegie libraries were built between 1883 and 1929 all around the world.

The teacher stopped the class on the front steps.

"Okay, you know what to do. Just remember to do it quietly," said the English teacher. "You have one hour."

It was a scavenger hunt the teacher devised as a teaching tool. Each student was given a sheet of paper with a set of numbers and letters at the top of the page, a Dewey Decimal Code, identifying a specific book. Each student was to find their number in the library card file, copy the title and author, then go to the corresponding stack of shelves, find the book, take it to one of the study tables and copy the first paragraph of page 12 of whatever book they found.

By now, the teacher knew each student so well that she chose books specific to the interest of the individual. Sally's book was 743.6 because she liked to draw. Jesse's was 782.82 because he loved to sing the classics. Montana's book was 636.9, *Safely Trapping and Tagging Wildlife*, because of her volunteer work at the Glen. Dale's book was about F. W. Morse, the inventor of the Morse code. Florence's book was 793.89 about Edgar Bergen, the ventriloquist, and Charlie McCarthy, his puppet, and William's was the biography of Scott Joplin, a famous jazz pianist William loved. Each student was delighted with their find, except today, Montana's book was nowhere to be found. They looked everywhere for 636.9, *Safely Trapping and Tagging Wildlife*, but it was missing. The librarian insisted it had not been checked out, so it had to be somewhere in the library.

"Look," whispered Florence, still clutching her Edgar Bergen book. Her eyes were on a man leaving the library.

"What?" said Montana.

"That's the guy that was watching us from the cliff."

"Are you sure? How can you tell?" asked Sally.

"I know. You just can't see it."

"The glow?" asked Montana.

"Yep."

The rest of the Wesley Club watched Vince Arledge go down the steps. Sally and Jesse went to the door and saw him get into the old rusty Suburban. Florence joined them and watched his menacing glow drive down Edison Boulevard.

"He is not a good person," Florence said.

Vince's Chevy Suburban

Max held the library book in his lap. "I didn't know you had a library card," said Max.

"I didn't need one today." Vince pulled onto US 68N to Yellow Springs.

"We're going back to the Mill. I've got to figure this out."

As Vince drove back to their apartment, Max thumbed through the pages of 636.9, *Safely Trapping and Tagging Wildlife.*

"It says here beavers mate for life. Do we take one beaver or the pair?"

"I'll have to think about that. Didn't you only see one?"

"It was too dark. They might have little beavers living with them. Will we trap them, too?"

"That eagle is sounding a lot easier all of a sudden," said Vince.

"Where's Mr. Van Wheaton going to put them once you trap them?"

"*Von* Wheaton, idiot! I guess he'll put them in that big barn of his."

Wednesday, May 14,1958, Noon
Central Junior High School Cafeteria

After the library scavenger hunt, the English class went directly to the cafeteria and, as usual, the Wesley Club sat at their table by the windows.

"Are you working tonight?" Sally asked Jesse.

"No, but I still have to babysit Christina."

"Janice is driving Dale, Montana, and me to the Glen to sketch and photograph birds for the pamphlet."

"How long will you be there?"

"Until seven, at least."

Jesse sighed. "I can't. Not tonight."

He played with his food as the rest of the club discussed what birds they would find and how many they needed for the new Glen Helen pamphlet. Jesse wasn't really listening. He wanted to go with the club and most of all, be with Sally while she sketched.

He thought of his mom and how, if she didn't have to work all day, he wouldn't have to babysit his sister. He thought about his dad and how, if he had just straightened himself out a long time ago and quit drinking and gambling, his folks wouldn't be divorced and his mom wouldn't have to work, and he could go help the rest of the Wesley Club do the Glen Helen pamphlet project.

Then Montana said, "I know this place where we can get a blue heron. And guess what? Sally, do you want to sketch a turkey vulture?"

"They are ugly," said Dale.

"Can I get a ride with you?" said Florence to Dale.

Jesse wondered if he could just go with them and take his sister, too. Maybe he could leave a note for his mom.

CHAPTER 5

Thursday, May 15, 1958, 4:30 p.m.
Glen Helen

Janice and Sally stationed themselves at the pond up Yellow Springs Creek where there were low hanging branches. An old log was the perfect bench.

"You'll see most of the Glen's birds around here," Montana told them. "Look! A great blue heron." She pointed east and all eyes followed. It was standing so still on a tree trunk in the middle of the pond. "I told you!"

Sally watched it through her binoculars. Janice zoomed in with her 35mm camera. *Click.*

Two wood ducks swam silently near the shore.

"I want so much to feed them," Sally said.

"I know. Me, too. Mr. MacCarthy said absolutely do not feed anything around here. Especially a flock of crows." As if on cue, they heard the caws from a group of black crows. Janice looked up and quickly snapped a picture.

"That's a murder," said Montana.

"A what?" asked Sally.

"A murder of crows. A flock of crows is called a murder." Montana was heading back up the trail.

Sally turned back to sketching the blue heron, occasionally using binoculars to get the details. "Hmm. A murder."

Meanwhile, Montana stopped at the oak tree with the eagle nest in it. The nest was easy to see. It was a huge collection of dead branches maybe a full foot or so thick and three feet in diameter. She used her binoculars to get a closer look. Then a large black figure landed on a limb supporting the nest and nearly stumbled into the nest. But it was not an eagle. It was a turkey vulture and hopped along the limb, never challenged by the eagles, who owned the home currently being trespassed.

She had to be sure. She slipped off her shoes and socks, looked directly up the tree determining which crevices would support her feet or hands for a vertical climb. Then she reached her right hand into the crevice left from a limb, pulled her body up, pushing with her left foot on the rough oak bark. Then she found another crevice for her left hand to hold and pushed up with her right foot. She reached over to the first limb, grasped it with both arms, pulled her legs up in an upside-down straddle and then maneuvered her body like a gymnast, arms now on one side of the limb and pulled her entire body up until she lay horizontal on top of it. She scooted herself toward the trunk of the tree so she could stand upright. She looked up at the big black bird above her and then over to the pond where Sally and Janice were still studying the birds well below her. It was so quiet.

The black vulture was just two limbs above her, still studying the nest. She wanted to scare it away somehow and just said, "Shoo, vulture. Shoo away." An instant later, the vulture flapped its wings and soared away, directly toward Sally and Janice where it landed across the path next to the pond. Montana watched Janice turn and photograph the ugly bird. She saw Sally edge closer, flip a page in her sketch book and start drawing the bird which was now more interested in a dead snake.

Montana continued her climb up the eagle's tree and positioned herself on the same limb where the vulture had perched. It was an odd view. The male eagle was there but it was sitting very still. He was alive because his head moved slightly as Montana got closer. She watched the bird's eyes and could tell that it was frightened and hurting, that it wanted help. She reached into the nest and some force seemed to hold the eagle in its position.

"What happened here?" she asked calmly, lovingly.

She looked over to the pond. Sally was still sketching the vulture, but Janice was gone. Montana looked around the area but could not see her anywhere.

"Montana?" Janice said from under the tree.

"Up here," Montana said. "Go get Grandpa. Something is wrong with the male eagle."

"How'd you get up there?"

"I climbed up. I think the eagle is hurt."

While Janice was getting Mr. MacCarthy, Montana studied the nest. Feathers were everywhere and there was blood on the edge of the nest. That would not be so odd because small animals were killed and carried up to the nest by the eagles for food. Suddenly, the eagle raised its head and then tried to stand. Montana did not move. "It's okay. I'll help."

The eagle's movement exposed an egg and the bird plopped back down on top of it and pulled its head in close to the body. "Okay. I get it. Where's your mate?"

After a moment a sound like a burp came from the bird's body. Slowly it opened its beak and then started screeching. *Screech! Screech! Screech!* It startled Montana and she instinctively moved back from the nest.

"She'll hear that alright," Montana said. The bird repeated its call.

Screech! Screech! Screech!

Montana looked around hoping the call would get the female eagle's attention. The eagle quit its screeching and was visibly exhausted.

"Montana, what's up?" Mr. MacCarthy yelled up from the base of the oak.

"One of the eagles is hurt. There's an egg. The female is missing. I caught a vulture messing with the nest."

"The female's probably looking for food."

"I hope so. But the male is definitely in pain."

"Will he let you touch him?"

"Maybe."

"Use your shirt and wrap it around your hand." Grandpa MacCarthy said. She took off her long-sleeved shirt, leaving her with just a t-shirt. She wrapped the flannel shirt around her left arm and reached over to the eagle.

"See if he'll let you touch his wing. Maybe, if he flies off, we'll know he's okay."

Screech! The eagle did not move. She lifted the wing up from his body and he stood up again, trying to move away. She could see that he was using one leg to prop himself up and the other leg was hidden by part of the nest. In all this contact, not once did he bite at Montana.

"I think it's his leg, Grandpa. Guess what! He's got two eggs."

"This is a mess," he said. "Where's that other bird?"

He stared up into the tree where Montana and the nest were. "Check his crop," he yelled up to her.

This time, she unwrapped the shirt from her arm and slowly reached her bare hand over to the eagle. She stroked the front of his neck, harder and harder.

"I think it's empty," she yelled. "Are you hungry, boy?" His beak opened but this time there was no sound.

By now, the tree was surrounded by most of the Wesley Club, along with Janice, Mr. MacCarthy, and a couple of hikers.

"He's got to be hungry, Grandpa."

"We have to move him," Mr. MacCarthy finally said.

Thursday, May 15, 1958, 9:00 p.m.
Baron von Wheaton's Barn

Once darkness fell on the Glen, Vince drove his Suburban from the old Grinnell Mill up Hyde Road to a gravel driveway leading back one quarter mile into an area of rolling pastureland until he reached the white barn. He backed the vehicle up to the barn as the large door slid open. Slowly he continued until the entire car was inside and the door was slid shut by Baron von Wheaton.

Max got out and opened the back of the van exposing a simple cage with a canvas bag inside it.

"Get your money out," said Vince to the ruddy German. "Feast your eyes on this."

"You got my beaver!" said the Baron.

"No. Better. I got your eagle. I need a couple days for the beaver," said Vince.

Baron von Wheaton stepped back and looked around the barn area. "I thought we said I needed the beaver."

"I know. I know. But wait till you see this bird. It's a beauty."

He pulled the cage close to the edge of the car. "Are all the doors shut?"

"Yes. It's tight as a drum. But I want that beaver!"

Vince reached into the cage and carefully transferred the bag onto the edge of the back of the Suburban.

"Are you sure it's alive? It's not moving." Baron von Wheaton looked apprehensive.

"It's alive alright. I saved its life."

He opened the top of the bag, reached in, and carefully pulled out a beautiful American Bald Eagle, its head shrouded in a mask that completely covered its eyes.

"I was scouting around for where I could put a trap for the beaver. It was 5:30 yesterday morning and this eagle flew right by me and as it was coasting along the ground this bobcat smacked it down from behind a tree. I was able to grab it up and take it to the Mill. In an hour it woke up."

"I chased the cat away," said Max.

"How serendipitous," said Baron von Wheaton flatly.

"And don't you worry about that beaver none. No sir. I have that all planned. Now, about that money."

"Is the bird hurt?"

"Not anymore. I saved it. Look."

Vince gradually removed the mask off the eagle and stood beside it. The bird looked around the poorly lit barn and flew up onto the center beam of the building. Then, it started screeching and screeching. It flew from beam to beam, screeching its heart out.

"It's beautiful." The Baron was visibly pleased. "How are you going to get the beaver?"

"Oh. I have that all planned. I'm building a trap. Don't you worry. I found plans for my trap. I'll get you two beavers. I just need a couple days. Now, about that money."

The eagle flew up to the highest point in the barn. It screeched three more times.

"I ordered parts to finish the trap. I need money to get them. You understand?" As the conversation went on, all eyes remained fixed on the eagle perched on the highest beam in the Baron's barn.

Reginald von Wheaton pulled out the wad of bills and peeled off ten twenty-dollar bills. "Here. You get the rest when we have those beavers. Now. How do we get you and your car out of here without losing that eagle?"

Thursday, May 15, 1958, 10:00 p.m.
Trailside Museum

After numerous calls to friends in town, Mr. MacCarthy found a jar of baby food and spooned it into the gullet of the eagle.

"I don't feel any broken bones. But he's hurting. Probably bruised from some kind of fight." Grandpa MacCarthy started setting some mice traps in the museum for the next day's food for the eagle. "When he flies across the room on his own, we'll know if he will be ready to go back in the wild."

"Do you think the eggs are okay?" Montana asked.

"Yes, as long as he's willin' to stay sittin' on them. He's takin' a liking to you." Grandpa's Scottish brogue got thick, as it did toward the end of the day.

"I shooed away that vulture." Montana was sitting just a few feet away from the makeshift indoor nest.

"We'll have to watch the nest in the tree and keep other fowl away from it. They'll be needin' it again." They both looked toward the door when they heard the crunching of tires on gravel outside. "That must be Janice to take you home."

"Are you okay, Grandpa?"

"I'm fine. I'll see you after school." There was a tap on the door, and then Janice walked in.

"How's the patient, Dr. Doolittle?"

"Ha! He still won't talk," said Montana.

"Florence's mom and dad said okay to her staying overnight tomorrow. Guess who was also eating supper with them?" She hesitated just a moment. "You know the guy that teaches adult Sunday school? You know. The cute one."

"Ah, you must be meanin' David Brown," said Grandpa MacCarthy. "He's a good lad. Wildlife and Fisheries."

"That guy. Why was he there?" asked Montana.

"He's building a garage onto her aunt's house in the evenings and weekends."

"Enterprisin' he is," said Grandpa.

"Anyway, we've got to go. I have to get home. You ready, Montana?" asked Janice.

Thursday, May 15, 1958, 11:00 p.m.
Baron von Wheaton's Barn

Screech! Screech! Screech!

Baron von Wheaton aimed the powerful flashlight to the top beam nearly 25' above the floor of his barn.

"Isn't he a beautiful creature, Fraulein," said the Baron.

"It's a she, from the size of it," said the woman beside him. The eagle remained on the beam.

"My guys worked hard for this one."

"You know it's against the law. They're protected by laws."

"I know, Fraulein. $1,000."

"Hmm," she said. "Are you feeding her?"

"So far, she's feasting on mice." He directed the light to a corner of the barn. "There's a nest over there."

"Mice are creepy," said the woman.

"I hate them. I thought I got rid of all of them but now my cat is missing. I put out poison last week."

"Rat poison?"

"Yes."

"Okay. I'll pay $1,000 for your eagle. You give it to me first, and if it does not die in thirty days, I will pay you the $1,000. Take it or leave it."

"Look at that eagle. It's perfect. Nothing is wrong with it."

"Nothing is wrong with it but there's plenty wrong with its food. Poison rat, poison bird." She turned to him. "Baron, why do you think they need protection? We're poisoning their food with DDT and rat poison. You know. You are what you eat."

The Baron aimed the light back up to the beam, but the bird was not there. He aimed it back to the rat nest in the corner of the barn just in time to see the bird glide along the floor and scoop up the rodent with its right talon. The beam of light was not quick enough to determine the ultimate destination of the raptor.

"Well?" said the woman.

"Let me think."

"Take it or leave it," she said and walked toward the door. "I'll call you tomorrow."

Frau Schmidt led the Midwest Falconer Society, a group of falcon trainers that did shows around the Ohio Valley for fairs, circuses, and amusement parks. Her interest in eagles was recent and started with an eagle she had nursed to good health and when she discovered there was a black-market interest in them, her greed took over where her love had begun.

CHAPTER 6

Friday, May 16, 1958, Noon
Central Junior High School Cafeteria

It only took five minutes for the Wesley Club to fully assemble at the lunch table by the cafeteria windows.

"You look happy," Dale said as Florence finally sat down at the table.

"I am. Daddy started his job at the furniture plant. They hired Mom, too. Mr. Wells found us a neat house. That means we're staying here. Oh. Guess what?"

"What?" Dale asked.

"Aunt Audrey is going on a date with David Brown, that Sunday school teacher at church," she said with a broad smile.

"I like him," Sally chimed in. Then she turned to Montana. "How's the eagle?" All eyes turned to Montana.

"He's still alive. We got him to eat some baby food last night. Grandpa's going to feed him some fish. Oh, guess who's getting thc fish for him?" Without waiting for a response, she turned to Florence, "Your David Brown. He works for Fish and Wildlife."

"Hmm," Florence smiled.

"Weren't there two eagles?" asked Jesse.

"Yep. Grandpa's convinced the female was poached."

"Poached?" asked Florence. She pushed her glasses up the bridge of her nose.

"Stolen. Trapped, or something like that," said Montana.

"I bet it was that guy watching us at the Glen," said Florence.

"Well, it's illegal to poach. It's illegal to even have an eagle. They're rare and protected. We need to find them," said Montana.

The members of the Wesley Club took on their lunch trays as William said, "Our second case?"

"The Poachers!" Montana said, and hit her fist on the table.

Other kids in the cafeteria looked at their table.

"We need to pray about it," said Florence. The table got quiet, heads bowed, and as half the cafeteria students watched, Florence whispered a prayer.

"God, please protect Mrs. Eagle and help us to find her. Please heal Mr. Eagle. Please protect their eggs. Finally, help us find the poachers so they don't hurt any more animals. Amen."

In an instant, her prayer was at the ears of God and the Wesley Club was ready to do all they could to save the eagles and find the poachers.

"Tonight, we're supposed to photograph the night animals. Who's in?" said Montana.

"Can I bring Christina? Mom works late," Jesse asked.

"I insist," said Montana.

"Me, too," said Sally. "This is going to be great. I can get a close-up sketch of Mr. Eagle."

Friday, May 16, 1958, 6 p.m.
Trailside Museum

Montana was already at the museum when Janice walked in with the rest of the Wesley Club, including Christina.

"How's the patient?" asked Janice.

"He won't eat. We force-fed him some baby food. Grandma and Grandpa will watch him while we get set up," said Montana.

Mrs. MacCarthy picked up Christina and gave her a hug.

"Do you want to help, little healer?"

The Wesley Club members were a bit surprised at her comment.

"The whole church knows about this little angel. Mr. Grimes calles her 'miracle girl,'" Christina whispered in Mrs. MacCarthy's ear, "Potty!"

"Okay, then, you can help me get this bird to eat his fish." She kissed her on the cheek. "You kids go about your business."

"Whose truck is that?" asked Florence. She was staring out the museum window into the parking lot. Sally and Janice joined her. Florence turned to them. "Someone in there does not glow good. I think it's the guys that were watching us the other night."

Mr. MacCarthy joined them at the window. "Are you sure?"

"Mr. MacCarthy, there is a bad glow through the windows. I promise," said Florence firmly.

"Well, let's find out," said Mr. MacCarthy. "Do you have your camera, Janice?" He then saw it hanging by the strap on her neck.

"Never mind. I'm blind." The girls laughed.

"Sally, you walk with me over to that old car while Janice snaps a picture from the front. When we get close, laugh like I told you a joke. Smile and wave at them. When Janice goes back to the Glen, we'll go back with her. Janice, try to get their faces."

"I'll try, but those windows are pretty dirty," she said.

The plan was executed and as they came back in, they were all laughing. Sally grabbed her sketch book.

"We waved at them, and they waved back like they knew us," she said, and started drawing eyes and nose and hair until she had a portrait of the guy. "Guess what," she said. "It's the guy at the library. Look."

As they looked at her sketch a BMW sports car pulled just beside the Suburban. After a moment Baron Reginald von Wheaton opened his door, looked around, and then got into the back seat of Vince's car.

"We've got one more," said Jesse, staring as the car door closed.

"I know that car," said Mr. MacCarthy. That's some big shot who bought the old Whiteflower farm on Hyde Road." The door slammed shut and Janice slowly walked near the Baron's car and snapped a shot of the Baron sitting in the car with the Arledge brothers.

Vince's Suburban

"How's that beaver trap?" the Baron asked as he slammed the door shut.

"It's been deployed. We'll be back here later to see if it worked," said Vince.

"Good, who's that?" he asked watching Janice walk around his car.

"She's a bird watcher. She's been taking pictures of the trees," said Max. "She's kind of cute."

They watched Janice walk to the entrance of the Glen and point her camera to a red headed woodpecker in a half dead pine tree. Then she disappeared down the steps to the Glen.

"Did you say there was another eagle?" asked the Baron.

"There are two eagles. The female is still out there," said Vince.

"You idiot. You got the female. That's the male." The Baron's thick forehead furrowed.

"Nope. We got the big one. That's the male." Now Max was insisting.

"Big eagles are females. The smaller eagle is the male."

"Are you sure?" said Max. "The one we got was pretty big. It has to be the male."

"Not with birds. Large, female. Smaller, male. Anyway, that's why I asked you to meet me here. Can you show me the nest?"

"Why do you need to see the nest?" asked Vince suspiciously.

"I need the male one, too. How quick can you get it?"

Vince was silent for a minute. "I have to put some stuff together. I need the weekend."

"I also need you to get that eagle you left in my barn into a cage. I sold it."

"Okay. I'll work on that tonight. I'll be over later."

"Perfect. I'll make sure there's a bonus for you once I get paid. I need that second eagle in a cage. Got it?"

He could see Vince's face and had second thoughts about making him face another eagle... or two.

"Haven't you had those wounds looked at? You look terrible."

"Don't worry about me. Just make this worth my while."

"Just get me those birds." He opened the door. "And the beaver, too. Don't forget the beaver." The Baron went directly to his car.

Both cars pulled out of the gravel lot and Janice started back up the stone steps to the museum.

CHAPTER 7

Friday, May 16, 1958, 4 p.m.
Glen Helen

Once Sally fully sketched out the drawing of the Aldridge brothers, Montana described the plan for capturing the images of the nighttime animals.

"We'll start with the bats." Eyes got wide.

"There are bats here?" asked Dale.

"Bats are everywhere. They come out at dusk, but here they have a couple favorite trees," Montana said as she led the group down the steps into the Glen. About twenty steps down she stopped everyone. She aimed her binoculars toward the far side of the dam.

"There's two old sycamore trees. See?" She pointed off to the left. "There's hardly any leaves on them because they are dying. From here you can see the openings in each one." She handed the binoculars to Sally first. "That's where they leave the tree. Hundreds of them come out at the same time. They swoop up into the sky and then head for the water behind the dam. Over there." She pointed at the body of water created by the dam.

"They go immediately to the pond there to get a drink. That's where I'll be." She slipped on a pair of pigskin gloves that fit tightly on her hands. "Once you get your photo of them coming out of the trees, come down to the pond where we were yesterday, and I'll make sure you get a closeup look."

They marched down to the pond where Montana stopped and told them to continue on up to the two sycamore trees. Montana remained beside the pond. As they approached the trees Montana studied the western sky and watched the darkness swiftly drift into the Glen. The moon was waning so all that could light the sky was the billions of stars and the few streetlights on Corry Street. Sally and Janice appeared like shadows, now staring up into the sycamores.

The shadows suddenly stepped back, ducked, recovered, and Janice's camera clicked as she caught the bats leaving their daytime home. Montana chuckled, then slipped off her shoes and waded into the pond. The water was a bit colder than she expected. The last time she did this was last summer on a 90-degree day. She shivered, took a deep breath, and stepped further toward the center of the pond. She stood still, oblivious to fish and minnows bumping into her legs, and smiled because the bats were now scooping up mouthfuls of water and then darting up into the air. Montana slowly raised a gloved hand just to the surface as a bat was scooping up its nourishment. Instantly it was nestled in the glove and Montana stepped back to the bank of the pond cooing at the bat. Sally and Janice walked back down the path to the pond. Sally shone the flashlight on the miniature mammal while Janice took close up shots with her camera.

"Got it? This guy is losing his patience," said Montana.

"One more." Janice adjusted the f-stop and shutter speed on her camera and clicked two more pictures.

"This is amazing."

"Janice, get ready for one more," said Montana. "Shine the light here."

Montana released her tender grip on the tiny bat, now holding only its tail while Janice filmed it flap its wings and escape her grasp.

"I can't believe we did this," said Sally, just staring into the space where she could hear the wisps of air move from the hundreds of bats searching out gnats, mosquitoes, and other flying insects.

Montana stood still in the pond as Sally and Janice were still awed by the experience that lasted all of three or four minutes.

"Shh." Montana suddenly said. "Where's Christina?" She tilted her head, listening intently. A sound was coming from somewhere around the pond.

"We left her in the museum," said Janice.

"I hear a baby. Listen." The three stood very still and could hear the distinct sound like a child whining. Sally aimed the flashlight at a spot that could be the source of the sound. There was a mound of twigs and limbs and mud in the center of the pond.

"That's the beaver house," said Montana still standing in the pond. She turned her head and edged herself closer to it. Then the whining repeated and was such a frantic sound that she was sure something was in trouble. "I can't tell where it's coming from."

"Look. Closer," said Sally and moved the beam closer to Montana, away from the beaver den. The water rippled right in front of her and Montana reached into the moving water, her hands still gloved for the bats.

"There's something here." The whining had stopped. She moved one step closer and lifted a clump of leaves and branches above the surface of the water.

"It's a cage. Look at the chicken wire," said Janice. She snapped a picture as Montana lifted the cage.

"It's a trap." Montana raised it higher and became face to face with a beaver, clinging to the wire, and the whining started again.

"It's okay, big boy. We've got you." She pulled the trap to the bank. Janice reached for it and dragged it onto land. Montana found the latch that held one side of the trap in place and released it. "Okay Mr. Beaver. Go home." He waddled out of the trap, looked around, then stared at Montana, bowed, or something like that, and slid into the pond. He swam a few feet, slapped his tail on the water and dove for the entrance to his house under the water.

"That was amazing. Nobody's going to believe this," said Sally.

"Yes, we will," said William. "We've been watching from the path. Dale went for a blanket when he saw you in the water. That was so awesome."

"I am freezing," said Montana and they all surrounded her, protecting her from the cool evening breeze until Dale showed up.

"Let's go. Mrs. MacCarthy has Ovaltine hot chocolate waiting for us. Your grandpa has a new project for us."

"Did you guys see the bats?" Sally asked.

"We saw it all. This is going to be one cool pamphlet. You saved the beaver, Montana!"

"I know." She started crying and the six bodies climbed the 100 steps to Ovaltine and bologna sandwiches.

Trailside Museum

"Oh girl, you need to change," said Mrs. MacCarthy as she removed the blanket from Montana. "Here, put these on."

Montana changed into dry clothes which were always on hand for situations like this. When she went to see the eagle, she was ecstatic.

"Grandpa, did you see the eagle? Come look!"

"That's why I sent the boys for you. What do you think. Can we cut him loose?"

Everyone went to the room and stared at Jesse and Christina stooped by the eagle and feeding him fish. The once sickly bird had suddenly improved so much that he could have been the emblem of any nation.

Janice took his picture. *Click.* The eagle flew up on the back of a chair and perched there, waiting for someone to get him back to his real nest. Sally immediately started sketching the magnificent bird.

"We've got to move his eggs back to the tree first," said Montana. Janice documented each and every step of moving the eagle back to his nest. First, Montana put her jacket on and placed one egg in each of the pockets. The kids accompanied her down the stone steps into the Glen, while Mr. and Mrs. MacCarthy remained in the museum.

"Leg up," she commanded, and William instinctively cupped his hands and lifted her high against the trunk of the oak tree.

They all watched her climb the oak as Sally shined the light on each limb and tree branch she used to reach the nest, thirty feet above the base. She took each egg and placed it at the spot in the nest she had memorized the day before. "Okay," she yelled down to Sally who then directed the light to the museum and flashed it three times.

Once they saw the prearranged signal, Mrs. MacCarthy opened the door and just a few seconds later Mr. MacCarthy released the eagle. It flew above the trees and though there were fears below that the bird was off to another place, Montana waited, expectantly, and seconds later smiled when Mr. Eagle landed on the nest, just next to where she was sitting.

"Hello Mr. Eagle. Welcome home," she said.

Friday, May 16th, 1958, 9:15 p.m.
Baron von Wheaton's Barn

Max Arledge looked down the twenty feet to the bottom of the barn as he edged his way across the main beam now only ten feet away from the female eagle. Vince and the Baron looked up at him and Vince aimed the powerful flashlight at the bird, convinced the brightness would prevent the bird from seeing Max on the beam.

"Don't make any noise, Max," said the Baron.

"Yeah, Max, you're doing good," whispered Vince.

The bird turned away from the bright light. Max was now just six feet away.

"Another two feet and you can net him," said Vince. "When you get him, just let the net fall onto the bales of hay. We'll get him in the cage down here," said Vince.

"Boys, it's not a him. It's a her," said the Baron, now an authority.

"Right, I forgot," said Vince.

Max edged the extra two feet he needed to swing the net and recapture the eagle. He held the net like he was seining for fish.

"Now, Max," Vince said. "Toss it. Now!" he said again.

Max looked down at Vince. Vince moved his light onto Max.

"Now!" Vince repeated.

Max tossed the seine net perfectly. Vince aimed the light back at the bird, but the bird was gone.

"Oh. Oh. Oh." Max cried from the beam. There was the screech from the eagle, now perched on another beam. As Max looked up, he lost his balance.

"Help!"

He fell the full twenty feet, directly on the bales of straw landing flat on his back.

Vince ran over to him.

"Are you okay?"

"I can't get up."

"We need to call an ambulance," said Vince.

"No, we can't be found with that bird." The Baron was pacing. Max began to sweat large cold beads on his forehead.

"He might die if we don't get him help." Vince could tell that there was no reasoning with the Baron and ran to his car, opened the back, and returned.

"I'll take him. Help me get him in the car," Vince insisted.

"Yes, right," sighed the Baron in relief. Both of them carefully placed Max in the back of the suburban. The Baron shut the back door of the car while Vince opened the barn door, got in the car and slowly pulled out of the barn.

Mrs. Eagle heard the door open, sensed the path to freedom and silently glided out the door before anyone could notice.

Friday, May 16th, 1958, 9:30 p.m.
Glen Helen Eagles Nest

"How's it going, Montana," asked Grandpa MacCarthy from the base of the huge oak tree.

"He's staying with the eggs. He'll be okay. I'm coming down."

As she scooted back from the nest there was a series of screeches, first calling up from the eagle and then from the sky. Montana waited a moment, then felt the whoosh of air as Mrs. Eagle joined her mate in the nest.

"Where have you been?" said Montana softly. "You had us worried."

Mr. Eagle stood up slightly to reveal the two eggs and then Mrs. Eagle turned to face Montana.

"It's okay. I'm leaving. You look fine."

"Grandpa, guess who's back?" Montana said as she climbed down the tree.

"What?"

"Mrs. Eagle. She's back home."

"Now I would have sworn she was poached!"

"What should we do with this?" Jesse asked. He and William were holding the beaver cage.

"Let me look at that." Grandpa MacCarthy studied it with his flashlight. "It's a trap alright. Poachers. Boys, take it up to the museum. Janice, we'll need to look at those photos. You guys get your pictures tonight and we'll look at them tomorrow."

"Grandpa, we're going to nap. We'll do the next batch of pictures at two a.m. when we can get the raccoons and the night birds."

CHAPTER 8

Friday May 16, 1958, 11:30 p. m.
Trailside Museum

When they got back up to the museum, Mrs. MacCarthy had more Ovaltine hot chocolate poured in old cups.

"Janice, you've got your dark room back. You and the girls sleep in there," said Mr. MacCarthy. The four girls grabbed their sleeping bags and hot chocolate and set up areas of the dark room to sleep.

"We need to wake up at two a.m. for some more animals," Montana said.

"What will we see?" asked Florence.

"We can't be sure, but I've seen raccoons, red fox, possum, skunk, deer, and maybe a bobcat. In the trees we might see an owl, a night heron, whippoorwill, mockingbird, the yellow breasted chat, and, uh, there are more. I'm too tired to think."

"I don't know why you're tired. You only played tag with a hundred bats, saved an eagle and a beaver so far," said Janice. "That eagle didn't look too good yesterday."

"We'll have to ask Jesse about the eagle. I think his sister had something to do with that. Where is she?" said Montana.

"Mrs. MacCarthy is taking her home to sleep in a real bed. We'll see her tomorrow," said Florence. They heard the door slam and a car drive out of the parking lot just as they spoke.

Jesse, Dale, and William studied the cage they had dragged up the steps.

"The screws are wacky," said William. "We won't be able to take them out. It needs a special screwdriver."

"Yeah, they're square instead of flat. A Phillips wouldn't even work on these," said Jesse.

"Hmm." Mr. MacCarthy leaned over the cage. "Those are Robertson screws. You won't find any of those around here. This is getting wacky alright. First the eagle miraculously recovers, then these fancy screws." The boys smiled at Jesse, and he held his finger to his lips.

"Maybe the trap was made in a foreign country," said Dale.

"Nope. It's handmade alright. Pretty recent, too. Let's get some rest. We'll noodle on this tomorrow. The girls will get you guys up at two o'clock."

Saturday May 17, 1958, 2:00 a. m.
Greene Memorial Hospital

"Thanks, nurse. I thought he was a goner when he fell," said Vince.

"If it was on a hard surface he'd be in bad shape. Broken bones for sure. A sprain can be fixed with aspirin and ice. For the next 24 hours these are best to ease his pain." She handed him a bottle containing four white pills.

The nurse helped Max into the car. "When these pills are gone give him a couple aspirin. He should lay down for a while. The ace bandage gives him support. You can stop wrapping him with it in a week. Goodbye, Mr. Smith."

"Uh... Our name..."

"Thank you nurse. Relax Max. I'll take care of you." Vince reached across Max's body, grabbed the handle, and pulled the door closed, his body leaning against Max's chest.

"Oohh," groaned Max. "That really hurt. Vince, our name isn't Smith."

"I know that. They don't need to know our real name. If the Canadian authorities know we are here, we'll have to go back to jail. We have a good thing going right now. Don't blow it!"

"Oh, yeah. Let's go home."

"We have to make a stop first."

"Where?"

"The Glen. I have to check the trap. Don't worry. It's on the way."

"Let's do it later, when you can see everything."

"The problem with that is everything can see back. We need that beaver. You can wait in the car if you want."

Saturday, May 17, 1958, 2:30 a.m.
The Pond at Glen Helen

Montana sat on a fallen log at the edge of the pond holding an unlit flashlight. Sally sat on the same log with a sketchbook in her lap while Janice exchanged the lens on her camera. Florence stood behind everyone and managed the canteen and bag of apples, their snack for the evening.

"Boo!" Came a voice from behind them. Florence jumped forward into the back of Montana.

"Stop it! You'll scare away the wildlife." Everyone could sense the disgust in Montana's voice.

"Sorry," said William.

"Shh. Look." She put her hand over the light and aimed it at the bank of the pond. She allowed just enough light for them to see an entire family of raccoons at the edge of the water eating on a single fish.

"Is that enough light, Janice?"

"I need a little more."

"How's that?"

Click. "Got it."

"How do they do that in the dark?" asked Dale.

"They have amazing eyesight at night."

Sally remained on the log watching and sketching.

"That's a good one," said Jesse. Sally turned her head up to see him and then stopped her gaze at the cliff.

"Who's that?"

"It's one of those guys watching us the other day," said Florence.

They all believed her. Montana turned off the flashlight.

The beam of the flashlight from the man on the cliff reached the beavers house in the middle of the pond and then moved. Then it was directed on the stone steps as the man and light slowly descended into the Glen.

"Let's move a little higher," said Dale. "This is too close."

As the man maneuvered down the 100 steps, the Wesley Club retreated up the Inman Trail another fifteen paces to the trunk of a large tree. The man stopped on the trail on the opposite side of the pond. The beam of his flashlight followed along the bank to a stake. He reached down and came back up holding a rope in his hand. He pulled on it, slowly at first, then much faster once he felt no resistance until the other end came up through the water, obviously not tied to anything.

"He's after that trap," whispered Jesse.

Now the man was staring directly at the beaver house in the center of the pond, both fists clinched, and his head bobbing up and down. Had they been able to see his face they would have seen tears of despair turn into determination. He sat on the bank, took off his shoes and socks and started wading into the pond.

"Montana, can you get your grandpa?" asked Jesse.

"Right. I'll be back. Wait here." She handed him her flashlight.

Silently, she made her way back down Inman Trail to Talus Trail leading toward the 100 stone steps to the museum.

The man waded to the edge of the beaver house, shining his light into the water, shifting his position a few steps one way, and then another, quickly covering a 20' radius from the beaver house.

Saturday, May 17, 1958, 2:45 a.m.
Pond at Glen Helen

Vince scratched his head with one hand and shined his flashlight with the other.

"It has to be right here," he whispered to himself.

Then he aimed the light at the far bank of the pond where the kids had been sitting just a few minutes before. He focused the light on one particular spot where they had dragged the trap onto shore.

"Somebody found my trap." All kinds of thoughts went through his head. He turned off his flashlight, stood silently, looked around, expecting to be arrested for illegally trapping a beaver.

Screech! Screech! The sound of the eagle startled him, and he turned toward the bank as the familiar eagle swooped down within five feet of him and skimmed the water with her talons and retrieved a blue gill fish.

Screech!

Twice Vince fell full face into the pond, tripping over branches concealed by water and mud.

A light beam from the cliff found him just as he crawled onto the bank. He scrambled around for his shoes just as another beam of light came from the opposite side of the pond.

Mr. MacCarthy yelled down. "You there. Stop!" Montana followed her grandpa down the steps as Vince headed north up Talus trail, and as Mr. MacCarthy descended into the Glen, Vince found a path back up to the parking area, jumped into the Suburban and peeled out onto Corry Street. Breathing heavily from the climb, he looked in the rear-view mirror to see two police cars, lights flashing, pull into the Glen Helen parking lot.

"Was the trap there?" asked Max.

"Did you see a trap? Did you see me put a trap in the back of the truck? Did you see me put a beaver in that bag and tie it up and put it in the truck? You're an idiot."

And Max remained silent from that point forward until they got to their apartment in the Grinnell Mill.

CHAPTER 9

Saturday, May 17, 1958, 3:45 a.m.
Trailside Museum, Glen Helen

When the police left, it was decided to delay any more outdoor work.

"I only got to sketch half the raccoon," said Sally. "Did you get photos?"

"Yes. This roll is done. Let's develop them."

"And then sleep. Okay?" said Jesse.

"You guys go ahead and get some rest. Dale and I will do the film and prints," said Janice.

"I'll help, too," said William.

They went into the dark room, cleared out the make-shift eagle nest, and started processing the roll of over thirty photos Janice had taken the last two days. Jesse went into the office area where the boys would sleep and crawled in his sleeping bag.

Sally, Montana, and Florence stayed in the Museum display area.

"Florence, how's your mom and dad?" asked Montana.

"They can't wait to get in a house. We move Monday."

"Where?"

"Close to Sally. Stadium Heights."

"What was it like? You know. Prison or jail." Montana sat up.

Florence was lying on her back staring at the ceiling. Silent at first, then a few seconds later she said, "I don't know, really. They don't want to talk about it I guess, and I've been afraid to ask. Mom and Audrey talked about some of it. Yesterday, Mom said things were going to be so different and better here."

"My dad was in a POW camp," said Montana. "I wonder if it was the same."

"POW?" said Florence.

"Prisoner of War camp. He was being held by communists in North Korea."

"Did he get out?" said Sally.

"Nope. At least that's what the army says. He died on some death march. Tiger death march. Grandpa says he was a hero. Sometimes, I..."

"What, Montana?"

"What if he really didn't die? They say there are still prisoners over there. He could be one."

"Maybe we could find out?" said Florence. "My dad was wounded in the Philippines. At least he came back."

"You are so lucky to have him with you. Mom died a year after my dad did. That's why I live with Grandpa."

"Do you remember them?" asked Sally.

"A little. When I was four, he'd take us into the Hocking State Forest. He would roll Mom in her wheelchair along this path and then he'd take her out and we'd sit on a blanket. I'd watch him climb rocks. We cheered him on. That's all I remember. He volunteered for Korea. I don't know why he did that. Florence, you need to talk to your dad about those times. I wish I knew more."

"Guess what?" Florence said.

Now Sally sat up. "What?" they both said.

"Daddy goes to Grandpa's to pick up his car."

"The Blue Studebaker Champion," Sally and Montana said at the same time.

"Mr. Gregory still says we solved that crime."

"All of a sudden, there were clues everywhere," said Florence.

"Maybe we can figure out who these guys are trying to steal my animals," said Montana.

"Can I help?" said a small voice.

Sally got up and turned the light on. Slowly, out of Florence's sleeping bag appeared her puppet.

"Paddles!" Montana said.

"We need to find out who wants to trap us beavers!" she said, Florence's lips not moving.

There was a knock on the door and then it opened.

"I can't sleep," said Jesse. "Your grandpa snores. Why are your lights on?"

"We're going to catch the poachers," said Paddles. "Do you want to help?" Jesse laughed and sat down on the floor next to Sally.

"Remember what we did first? We wrote down everything we knew about the case," said Jesse.

"Okay, let's get started." Sally opened her sketch pad to a plain piece of paper.

"Let's nab those guys!" said Paddles.

Sally printed on the page a big numeral one.

"That's a start," Jesse said, and they all laughed.

"The climber things. That thing with the spike," said Montana. "Grandpa still has it."

Jesse looked confused.

"You weren't there. We found this spike they use to climb trees on that pine that fell next to the eagle's nest," Montana said. Sally wrote down: *Climber Spike.*

"How about the trap you rescued the beaver from," said Jesse. "It had those weird screws."

"Robinson screws," said Montana.

"Robertson screws," Jesse corrected her.

"Yes, yes. Robertson screws. Grandpa said they use them in Canada."

Sally wrote down *Trap with Canadian* screws behind the number two. Montana took the sheet and taped it on the wall.

Then the door to the dark room opened.

"What are you guys doing?" asked William.

"We couldn't sleep," said Florence.

"What's this?"

"Clues. We need to find out who's poaching the animals," said Montana.

"Look in here if you want clues," said William.

Janice was hanging the 8 x 10 photos she had developed from her roll of film on a length of string spanning the room.

"Look at the raccoons!" Montana said. "These are perfect, Janice." One raccoon was drinking while another one was washing its hands.

"The blue heron looks so majestic," said Paddles, and all the kids laughed.

"There was this mist and the camera caught it just right," said Janice.

"That's the guy!" said Florence, suddenly. They all were drawn to a photo of the dirty Suburban with a profile of Vince looking in the backseat, his hands captured in some kind of gesture, the mouth open, and the eyes wide with some kind of excitement.

"I wonder what they were talking about?" asked Jesse.

"Our eagle, I bet," said Florence.

"Janice! You got their license plate. Alberta. Where's that?" asked Dale.

"It's out west in Canada. I've been there," said Montana.

"Those screws are from Canada, right?" yelled Sally, now from the museum display room. She was writing, *3. Photo of suspects' car with Canada plates* on the clue list. Then she wrote, *4. Photo of suspect.*

"This is another clue," said Janice. She pointed at the photo of the shoe print they found on the bank of the Yellow Springs creek.

"What?" yelled Sally from the other room.

"A shoe print of the suspect," Dale yelled back.

"Shh. You'll wake Mr. MacCarthy," said William while Sally wrote *5. Shoe Print.*

Sally continued writing, *6. Suspect glowed.* "We might have to explain that one," she said softly to herself.

"We need a photo of those screws," said Jesse.

"I got it when Montana saved the beaver," said Janice. "It's on that string over there." She pointed to another line of at least a dozen photos drying near the wall.

"Look at this," Janice said. She was staring at the photo she took when Vince fell face first into the water and caught him struggling to stand back up. "He's bald on the back of his head."

"What's that he's holding?" Florence asked.

William grabbed up a magnifying glass and studied it. "I think it's hair. He wears a .." He was suddenly at a loss for words.

"A toupee!" said Dale. They all gathered around the photo and laughed.

"Don't you kids know what time it is?" They turned to see Mr. MacCarthy standing by the door to the dark room. "What's this all about?"

"We're collecting clues, Grandpa. We have to stop the poachers," said Montana.

His hands were on his hips. He stared at the two strings holding photographs in the dark room, then back at the two sheets of paper now taped to the wall with the list of clues.

Suddenly, there was a crunch of tires outside the museum. Dale looked out the window and could only see the red taillights of a vehicle pull out of the parking lot. They ran outside. The only cars in the lot were Janice's and Mr. MacCarthy's.

"Could you tell what kind of car it was?" asked Mr. MacCarthy.

"No, sir. It headed down Corry Street." He pointed south into the darkness.

Mr. MacCarthy walked around the building. "He got what he came for. That trap is gone."

"Oh no," said Dale.

"We still have the picture," said Janice.

"What?"

"I took a picture of it." He looked around at the Wesley Club surrounding him and Janice and shook his head. "I don't believe it. I just don't believe it. You all are remarkable."

Saturday, May 17, 1958, 4:00 a.m.
Grinnell Mill Apartment

"The way I look at it, Max, is that trap worked. I just didn't pick it up soon enough," Vince said.

"Are we going to put it out again?"

"Let me think. They can't be the only beavers around here."

"How can you find out? Maybe ask the Baron?" said Max.

"Oh, no. Let me think."

He stared out his window to the Little Miami River flowing by.

"There has to be more beavers," he said out loud.

"But where?" said Max.

"We're going on a hike once the sun comes up. Let's get some rest."

"Why don't we just go back to Canada. It wasn't as complicated there," said Max.

"And get arrested, you idiot! They have our pictures everywhere. That's why the Baron suggested we come here for a while."

"Who do you think took your trap?"

"Probably that museum guy. He's always checking on those beavers."

CHAPTER 10

Saturday, May 17, 1958, 5:30 a.m.
Yellow Springs Creek at Grinnell Road

Vince could barely see the sun rise because of the trees along the creek bank. He followed animal trails along the winding creek, stepping over small tributaries that feed the creek just before it emptied into the Little Miami River. He stopped for a moment to see three deer drinking from the water and then vanish quietly into the woods. The creek wound its way toward Grinnell Road and Vince continued through the culvert to the other side which put him back into the Glen Helen Reserve and it was there, within one hundred feet of the culvert that he saw what he was looking for -- a small wet area created by a beaver dam.

He walked along the edge of the thousands of limbs, twigs, and mud that made up the dam. It was just twenty feet of dam that turned the soaked soil on the other side mucky. Two small trees had already been cut down by the toothy rodent and lay on the ground ready for the next evening's work shift.

Then he saw their tracks. There was more than one beaver, which is normal. But, as far as he was concerned, he only needed one beaver to satisfy the Baron. There, just beyond the bend of the creek, under the overhang of mud and grass, there, the tracks led, and there, that was where the trap would be set. He climbed up the bank and slowly turned, watching for any sign of the one animal he needed to avoid just now. Humans. Then he pulled the binoculars out of the case hanging from his neck. He repeated the move, slowly turning and peering through the lenses, the full 360 degrees, stopped, dropped the glasses in the case and started assembling the beaver trap. It was a simple trap, the beaver, leaving its den, would have no choice but to enter the cage and after being about one foot inside the trap would have to step on the panel that released the hinged door that simply swung down and blocked the beaver's escape.

Saturday, May 17, 1958, 8:00 a.m.
Trailside Museum

"Jesse, it's time to get you back to Xenia." Mrs. MacCarthy's voice finally drew Jesse from his deep sleep.

"Hi, Jesse," said his little sister Christina. "Home. Now."

It was Saturday and Jesse had a full day to put in at Pat's Market.

"What time is it?" he asked, sitting up and rubbing his eyes.

"Eight in the morning. That's when you wanted to get up. Mr. MacCarthy is ready to take you home. Roll up your bag."

"Yes, ma'am." He stretched.

"Jesse, home," repeated Christina.

"We'll see you at church, Jesse," said Dale.

"Bye, Jesse," said Sally.

Jesse and Christina left the rest of the Wesley Club to work on the pamphlet.

Mrs. MacCarthy opened a picnic basket, and the aroma of bacon and egg sandwiches filled the room and woke up the rest of the Wesley Club. "You need to eat before you go out in the wild again, kids."

"Yum." Sally chewed on the breakfast sandwich.

"Coffee or orange juice?" said Mrs. MacCarthy. "Mr. MacCarthy wants you to be ready for when he gets back. Do you have your lists worked out?"

"Yes, Grandma. We still have six birds to find, including a couple owls."

"We need to find that fox, an otter, and a bobcat."

"Don't forget the skunk," said Dale.

"Yuck."

"Okay, kids, call your folks and check in."

Saturday, May 17, 1958, 1:00 p.m.
Grinnell Mill Apartment

Simultaneously, Baron von Wheaton's BMW roadster and Vince's Suburban pulled into the Grinnell Mill driveway. Vince remained behind the wheel of his car and cranked down the window as the Baron limped over.

"You let my eagle out. Give me back my $200. You're through."

"What? That eagle was in your barn last night."

"Well, guess what flew out when you tore out of there with your brother? The eagle." There was an angry vein throbbing on his temple.

"That's not my fault. Listen. I'm going to get you a beaver by tomorrow and then I'll go back and get them eagles. I did it once, I can do it again. Trust me. I'll get both them eagles."

"Guess who called me after you left last night?"

"Now how am I supposed to know who called you?"

"You know that Field and Stream reporter? He's working a story about poaching in, guess where?"

"Baron. I can't read minds."

"Ontario. He specifically mentioned Southwold Earthworks and a roomful of missing artifacts. Is that where you got them flint tools you sold me? Well, they don't know I have them yet."

"You're okay. You're in the U.S. now. No jurisdiction," said Vince. He was gripping the steering wheel.

"Reporters have jurisdiction everywhere. If they ever find out, U.S. and Canada will start cooperating all over the place."

"Baron, I already set my beaver trap. I'll get you the eagle, too."

"Eagles! Two eagles!"

"All right. But there better be another ... Uhm $300 in it for me."

Baron von Wheaton turned and walked to his car.

CHAPTER 11

Saturday, May 17, 1958, 1:15 p.m.
Grinnell Mill Apartment

"Was that the Baron?" asked Max from his bed.

"Yeah. We have to move fast now."

"Where to?" said Max.

"No, you idiot. We have to get two eagles and a beaver quick."

Vince sat down on the seedy chair.

"First. That eagle flew out of the barn when I took you to the hospital. The Baron wants it back." He stared out the window "He wants his money back."

"You said, 'first.' Is that all?"

"Somebody's tracking those Indian flints we found in Ontario. They were part of a collection. Somehow, they know about me selling them to the Baron."

"Why don't we just move and go someplace else, then. I don't trust that Baron."

"He's okay. As long as I get him what he needs. Two eagles and a beaver. Can you walk? I need to scope out that nest again. I bet I have that beaver before midnight. My trap will work. I know it will." Vince looked at his watch.

"What if it worked already?" Max said.

"You mean my trap?"

"What time did you put it out?"

"It was about six this morning." Vince checked the time again.

Max got out of bed. "I'll help. How far away is it?"

Vince helped him get dressed.

"It's close to the culvert up the road. Okay, look, you drive. Drop me off at the culvert. I'll check the trap." Vince stared out the window. "See that 'narrow road' sign up there?" Max looked without saying anything. "The yellow one. See it?"

"Right."

"Watch for me. I'll come up to the road and wave. Then you come pick me up."

"Right."

"Are you sure you can drive?"

"Let's go," said Max as he slowly walked to the door.

Vince grabbed the brown canvas bag he had used to transport the eagle and got in the passenger side of the car. Max slowly got into the driver's side. After a minute of adjusting the seat and the mirrors, he started the car.

It was a Saturday afternoon and traffic on Grinnell Road was heavy with Glen visitors, John Bryan State Park campers, Antioch College students, and local farmers. Max stopped the car at the culvert and Vince grabbed the bag and slipped out as cars lined up behind them. Once the passenger door was shut, the car pulled away and Vince edged down the steep bank into the southern tip of Glen Helen. He followed the creek to the exact spot where he had set the trap and was relieved it was still there covered by twigs and limbs.

Then he heard the whine, like a baby, and he grinned. He opened the bag, set it aside, lifted the camouflage of limbs, and revealed a beautiful beaver. It whimpered as he unlatched and opened the top, grabbed the beaver by the scruff of its neck and dropped it in the canvas bag, carefully tying it shut with a double knot. He looked over the cage, amazed as to how easy this was without those kids messing with his trap. He could have collapsed it right there and removed it, along with the bagged beaver but then he remembered Max reading from the book at the library, *It says beavers mate for life.*

It only took Vince two minutes to reset the trap, reposition it in front of the beaver den on the creek bank, and replace the camouflage of twigs and limbs. He grabbed the bag and went back up the bank onto the side of the road. He looked down the road to the Grinnell Mill and waved. A white Studebaker stopped.

"Get in," said the driver.

"It's okay. My ride is back there." Vince said, holding the bag with the beaver behind his back with one hand and pointing toward the mill with the other.

Twice, drivers stopped to give Vince a ride, and twice, he refused. He finally started walking toward the mill which was only a half mile down the road. The beaver whimpered inside the bag and to Vince, the sound was so loud that the cars that passed him must have heard it. Every time a car passed, he instinctively put the bag behind him. When there were no cars in sight, he waved again toward the mill.

"Where is that idiot!" he said, multiple times. "He can never do anything right."

As the trees cleared to his left, he could now see the entire mill and the Suburban was just sitting there. He looked around. There were no other vehicles around him. As he got closer, he could see Max sitting on the driver's side. He walked faster and finally crossed the road to find Max sound asleep behind the wheel. He pounded on the window.

"Wake up, you idiot!"

Max startled awake and then rolled down the window.

"Move over. I've been waving up there for five minutes." Vince opened the back of the car and carefully set the bag with the beaver down. He slammed the back door shut and got into the driver's side.

"What's wrong with you. You had one job!"

"Sorry, Vince. I think it's those pills they gave me at the hospital."

"How many did you take?"

"They said take one every four hours, but I took two, it was hurting so bad."

"Does it hurt now?"

"I don't feel a thing."

"I bet you don't. Don't mess with that stuff. That's what got Mom and Dad split up. Narcotics. They'll take away your pain, but they'll kill you if you're not careful.

"Did you get it?"

"Yep. It's a beaut! That Baron's gonna pay plenty."

"Where's the trap?"

"There's another beaver down there. We'll check the trap again later. Now let's get this over to the Baron's farm."

Saturday, May 17, 1958, 3 p. m.
Trailside Museum

"I'm sorry, kids, but we have to cancel today. There's too much wind. We stop the hikers because our trees are unpredictable. They'll drop limbs without warning," Mr. MacCarthy said.

"Bummer," said Janice.

Just then a gust of wind shook one of the windows facing the parking lot. The force of the rain was so intense, they all stared at it, expecting it to blow in.

"Let's use this time to see where we are with the pamphlet." Mr. MacCarthy described the association's expectations with a list he had in his notebook. "Let's check off what we have. Mind you, we don't need all these animals. If we get a good variety and great images everyone will be quite happy."

"Okay, I'll write down the ones we still think we need." Sally placed a numeral '1' on the left-hand top side of a blank sketch sheet.

"Ground Squirrel," he said.

"Check," said Montana.

"Raccoon."

"Check."

He continued reading off bird names and animals. The list was extensive but even the kids were amazed at how many they had managed to get images of. Thirty-five, so far.

"Grandpa, we for sure need that woodchuck near the Pine Forest. There's the red fox by the Mill. I think the bobcat has a den in one of the caves by the gorge. I saw a badger by the Hopewell Indian mound."

"That would do it for the mammals. Eagle?"

"Check." They all laughed.

"Blue heron."

"Check."

He continued down the extensive list, sometimes having to repeat himself after a loud burst of rain drowned out his voice.

"We need a few more birds. What do you suggest?"

"I keep seeing this hawk or something flying around the school forest," said Janice.

"I know how to get her. I know where the nest is. It's by the gorge," said Montana.

They discussed the great horned owl, yellow-bellied sap sucker, and red-headed woodpecker, among others and then the door to the museum opened and a man covered in a wet rain slicker walked in and stomped his feet.

"Can I find some coffee in here? Hey kids." David Brown's hair was disheveled despite the rain hat he had just hung on a hook in Mr. MacCarthy's office.

"Hi, David." Florence was the first one to speak.

"What brings you here, son?" said Mrs. MacCarthy as she handed him a mug of coffee. "There's milk in the fridge."

"This rain interrupted my garage building, so I thought I'd check out how the pamphlet is going. What's going on with the Wesley Club?"

"Ah, they're almost done. We have a few pesky animals to find and finish up. Show him the list, Sally," said Mr. MacCarthy.

"This shouldn't be too difficult. What's this?" David walked over to the photos and drawings laid out on one of the museum display cases.

"These are the images we're going to use so far," said Florence. "Sally drew these."

"How did you get the bat?" He held up the sketch and compared it to Janice's photo of Montana releasing the bat from the pond.

"Miss Doolittle did it all," said Janice, smiling at Montana. "She waded in the water and just waited for one of them to get a drink next to her. I think she talks to them. That was the night she saved the beaver from the trap."

David looked at Mr. MacCarthy wide-eyed. Then he looked at Montana.

"Where did you learn to do all this, Montana?"

Before she could say anything, Mr. MacCarthy answered.

"Her mom and dad. Her mom, especially. She would walk in the woods for hours with the infant Montana on her back. That's why my son fell in love. He wanted someone who liked the outdoors."

"I just know the animals. They know me. We're friends," Montana said. She looked at her grandpa and he smiled warmly.

"Ah. David. Have you ever heard of a beaver trap made with Robertson screws?" asked Mr. MacCarthy.

"I like those screws. Too bad we don't have them here. The trap must be made in Canada or Europe."

"I think it was made here by a Canadian. Janice, where's those pictures." Janice went into the dark room and brought back the yellow envelope with the pictures she took of Vince, the trap, and the vehicle.

"It looks handmade to me. I think these are all related," said Mr. MacCarthy.

"These guys have bad glows, David," said Florence.

"You've seen them?"

Then the Wesley Club started describing the man wading and falling all over the pond trying to recover his trap which Montana had already removed. The laughter overwhelmed the pounding rain outside the museum when they showed him the one with Vince and his hairpiece.

"What's this?" David was now holding the photo of the BMW sports car. "I've seen this guy. This is that German guy that bought the Whiteflower place." He shuffled through all the photos and set out four and asked Janice if she could make copies for him. She went immediately into the darkroom, found the negatives, and printed the pictures.

"So, what's your plans to photograph the skunk?" David asked. Everyone looked at Montana.

"They're everywhere. All we have to do is be very still. It's easier than you think," she said.

"Tell that to Jesse." Dale went on to describe Jesse's encounter with skunks a winter ago at Camp Birch. "They made him stand on his clothes naked in the shower and soaked him with tomato juice to get rid of the stench and it was in the winter."

"Yuck!"

"That'll build some character, I'd say," said David.

"They're drying now," Janice said when she came out of the dark room.

Saturday, May 17, 1958, 3:00 p.m.
Baron von Wheaton's Barn

The Baron, Vince, and Max stood around the table under the single light in the vast barn. Vince set the canvas bag on the table, untied the top, nudged it on one end and the three gazed as the brown beaver inched its way out of the dirty bag. Then it stopped, as if it knew it was in the spotlight. Vince looped a wire around its neck and kept it centered on the table. It whined like a baby. The Baron smiled.

"Ah, my little engineer. You're going to build me a dam." The Baron leaned over it possessively with his hands firmly on the table.

"Hold him there Max, while I get the cage."

It was a small cage; a frame of two-by-two lumber screwed together with those Robertson screws and surrounded by simple chicken wire. The end was hinged. He placed the cage on the table and grabbed the beaver by the scruff of the neck and slid it inside the cage. He put three twigs full of leaves inside, with the beaver and a larger branch with plenty of bark on it. Then he slipped in a dog food dish and filled it with water.

"He'll have a helper really soon," said Vince.

"Another beaver?" asked the Baron with a grin full of jagged teeth.

"I'm hopin'. There has to be a family on that bank. Now. $1,000 for both eagles. How much for the beaver?"

"We'll talk about all that when you get those eagles."

Vince looked annoyed.

"That will be soon." There was a flash of light visible between the slats of the barn and then fifteen seconds later a rumble of thunder that lasted for another five seconds. "The storm's passing. C'mon Max, we've got more work to do."

Max limped behind Vince and got in the passenger side of the car while Vince opened the sliding barn door.

They drove back to Grinnell Road and turned left toward the Glen but continued on to Xenia Avenue and then right onto Route 343, where Vince pulled the car off the side of the road into a driveway that led toward a farmhouse.

"How are you doing Max? Can you walk? It's quite a hike."

"It hurts a little. I took my last pill an hour ago."

"Okay, that's good. Those things are bad for you anyway." A gust of wind blew through the trees, bending branches, exposing the silver leaves, and then there was a snap, and a large branch fell just next to the farmhouse. They both stared at the tree, expecting another branch to fall.

"I don't think anybody lives there. I'll pull the car up next to the house."

"Max, no one's gonna be in that Glen as long as it's windy like this. The sun's not coming out anytime soon. I need to get up to that nest. Let's go. Follow me." Max hobbled along behind him.

He opened the back of the Suburban and pulled out a canvas backpack full of gear. He strapped it on his back and the two started their hike down narrow trails ultimately connecting with Talus Trail, the trail that would lead them back to the oak tree with the eagle's nest. As soon as they made it to the oak tree, the sky let loose with a heavy downpour accompanied by rain and thunder.

"This is perfect," said Vince. "Both those birds will have to be there."

He pulled out one canvas bag from the pack. He checked inside to be sure the seine was there. He attached one end of the rope to the bag and the other end to his belt. The second canvas bag was inside the first, along with a pair of leather gloves used by falconers. Finally, he pulled a climbing rope with a grappling hook out of the pack. It took three tries for him to throw the rope high enough for the hook to reach the first limb of the tree. He'd use it again if he needed to climb the next twenty feet to the eagles' nest.

In the meantime, the Yellow Springs Creek kept rising, overflowing the dam in two different places. Max stayed close to the trunk of the oak tree which kept the bulk of the rain off him. He noticed how the creek, where he had nearly drowned, was now above the bank and nearing the Talus Trail.

“Max, you stay there. When I get up there and get the eagles, I’ll place them in the bag and lower them with this rope.”

CHAPTER 12

Saturday, May 17,1958, 4:00 p.m.
Baron von Wheaton's Barn

Baron von Wheaton's barn was the perfect place to keep an eagle or two as long as no one opened the barn door. The Baron asked Fraulein Schmidt to meet him and wait with him while Vince and Max recaptured the eagle.

"How do you know they'll be here? You've already lost one eagle."

"I know. They are both idiots, but when it comes to capturing animals, they are certified to be the best. Come over here." The Baron directed her over to the far wall of the barn where, on a table, sat the cage with the beaver, huddled in the corner of it and a bare branch at its side.

"Look at that pelt," she said.

"That's my engineer. He's going to build me a dam."

"You're not serious."

"It was going to cost me $2,000 and take six months to get my dam built by a human. This little fella will do it in just a month or so."

"You don't say."

"And then, I'm sure I'll get a pretty penny for him once he's finished."

"They are never finished."

"What?"

"They build the dams out of twigs and mud. The dam constantly needs repair. You know, busy as a beaver? Baron, I could have gotten you that beaver myself for $150. How much are you paying the Arledge boys?"

The Baron, now annoyed and confused, was suddenly deep in thought. He stepped away from the table and pivoted around to the barn door. There was the crunch of tires and the brief honk of a horn.

"Ah. My eagle, I hope," said the woman.

The Baron opened the barn door and the Suburban backed in as a flash of lightning momentarily lit the room. The exhaust from the car flowed in with the gust of wind and seemed to settle on the Baron and his friend. They each backed away and Vince took his time pulling the vehicle in. Stop. Go. Stop. Go. Gunning the engine each time. The woman started coughing first and moved toward the door and the rainy wind blowing in. The Baron waved his arm once the car cleared the door. He reached over to slide the barn door closed.

"Tell him to turn the engine off," the woman yelled between coughs.

"Turn the engine off!"

"What?" yelled Vince. He cranked the window down.

"Turn the engine off! You're killing us."

The engine stopped after a couple kicks from cheap gas.

Max was still getting out as Vince opened the back of the car.

"Stop," said the woman. "We have to get this stench out of here."

Vince looked confused and sniffed the air while the Baron went to the barn door and slid it open, allowing the rain and fresh air in. Vince shrugged his shoulders and stood by the back of the vehicle.

"Put the bag on the table by that beaver," said the woman. "Don't open it yet."

She looked surprised as Vince carried two canvas bags to the table by the barn wall.

"Now, drive the car back outside. No more accidents."

Vince did as she directed, and the Baron stood by the door while Vince cut the engine and came back inside the barn.

"Very well. Let's proceed."

The Baron shut the barn door and joined the three back at the table.

"I see two bags," the woman said.

"Yes ma'am. I have brought the Baron, yes, two eagles. Voila." He made a big show of it as he and Max untied the bags.

"Don't let them out."

The woman clamped a makeshift perch onto the table. She then put on a leather glove, pulled two hoods from her bag, and carefully attached them to each of the eagles.

"Here, put this jess on her talon." She handed the leather bird leash to Vince who attached it to the bird. They repeated the process for the male eagle.

"It's one thing to see an eagle, but to see two majestic birds side by side is amazing." The woman took multiple Polaroids of the two birds and then a close up of each one.

Sunday, May 18, 1958, 9:30 a.m.
Trinity Methodist Church

"Good morning, Methodist youth," said Mr. Wells. "I have news for you. All fourteen of you will continue through the summer and next year with us. You will remain together so there is no more boys or girls Sunday school."

There was a mixture of responses, but the Wesley Club looked at each other smiling, except for Montana.

Mr. Wells stepped behind her and tapped her on the head and she jerked upward, suddenly wide eyed. "Are you okay, Montana?"

"Sorry Mr. Wells. We were up last night trying to find our eagles. We have poachers, Mr. Wells."

"Eagles?"

"You know, like the one that landed in the tree at the picnic last week. It's gone. They're both gone."

"Oh, no," said one student.

"What are you going to do?" asked another.

The entire class was focused on Montana.

"Maybe they found another nest."

"Not and leave these." At the same time, Sally and Montana lifted their arms revealing a sock shaped pouch hanging under each left arm.

"Eggs," said Dale. "The birds left their eggs."

Some kids got out of their chairs to get close to real eagle's eggs.

"Grandpa is looking for an incubator. Until then we're keeping them warm."

"What about the Atwell Turkey farm?" said Mrs. Lane.

"Hmm. We'll ask David after class. Keep the eggs warm, girls," said Mr. Wells.

"Now, about your gifts, some of you are quite aware of how you can use your gifts in the church. Florence, good news, Pastor Armey is hoping you can do the children's message at least once a month. He would like Paddles to help."

Florence smiled because it was already her wish, and it was coming true.

He then described other opportunities and the rest of the class helped each other think of ways their gifts would benefit the church. At 10:30 most of the kids had ideas of their contributions and it was time for church. Mr. Wells escorted Sally and Montana to David Brown's class.

"An incubator? I'm sure we can find one," he said.

"We were thinking about Atwell's Turkey farm. Would he have something like that?"

"Hmm. Actually, he has something better. Turkeys. Wait here."

He went to the church office and called Mr. Atwell.

When he returned to his classroom, he was smiling. "Mr. Atwell agreed to help us. See if your folks will let you go with me to his turkey farm after church.

Sunday, May 18, 1958, 12:00 p.m.
Trailside Museum

After church, Janice took William, Dale, Jesse, and Christina to the Trailside Museum while David took Sally, Montana, and Florence to the Atwell Turkey farm.

Janice and her team worked on the photos they already had and the sketches Sally had done. Some sketches had to be reduced in size to fit the space set aside for that particular animal. Janice took a photo of the sketch and then printed it to the size needed for the pamphlet. Since they had two-thirds of the pictures and sketches they needed, today's work meant the pamphlet was close to being finished.

"We've made some real progress here," said Mr. MacCarthy. Just then, David and his team walked into the museum.

"Okay, Robert, they're all yours. Mission accomplished. Any coffee here?"

"In the office. It's a tad old."

"What did you do with the eggs?" asked Jesse.

"You won't believe this," said Florence.

"When we got to the farm, Mr. Atwell took us into this long building. He went to this area where this turkey was sitting on her nest, but it was totally empty. He said she was 'broody.' He shooed her away, put the eggs in the nest, and then we went to the other side of the building and watched that turkey hop back in the nest and sit on those eggs. He told us not to worry about the eggs. He'll check them every day."

CHAPTER 13

Sunday, May 18, 1958, 1:00 p.m.
Shawnee Park

The photos were laid out on a sheet of paper, glued to the page, and captioned. *Auction, minimum $750 each*, and a phone number, printed by hand under the photos. Beside it was a stack of ten hand-made copies.

"Can you get these out tomorrow? We'll do the auction in your barn. I hand printed these so there is no paper trail," said Frau Schmidt.

"What are these photos?" The Baron pointed at pictures of smaller birds.

"Falcons. A total of five birds with your eagles. We'll do the auction on Wednesday."

"Why did you want to meet here? We could have met at the barn."

"We shouldn't be seen together near your farm too often. It could raise suspicion. During the day this park is the perfect place. Our business is too important. Here's a list of where they need to go."

"You're probably right, Liebchen. Let me have the copies."

"This one's mine," she said.

Sunday, May 18, 1958, 2:30 p.m.
Trailside Museum

"So, it looks like you need an otter, a bobcat, an owl or two, and a skunk," said David.

"I can do a skunk from a magazine if you want," said Sally.

"That might be cheating. Right Robert?" said David.

"Whatcha got in mind?" said Mr. MacCarthy.

"How long do we have?"

"Another couple hours."

"Okay, let's see what we can do with that. Get your gear kids then let's hop in the truck."

It took David less than ten minutes to drive to the Clifton Gorge. He parked at the side of the road and led the Wesley Club down a path that ended at the base of a cliff nearly thirty feet high. The cliff was kind of terraced. In fact, you could climb it by zig zagging up the face of it.

"This way." He took them away from the cliff about thirty feet, looked around and checked the wind direction by watching the leaves, stopped the team at a specific log, and then sat down.

"Dale, you guys watch up on that ledge, halfway up the cliff. Florence, keep your eye on that fallen tree over there. Wait here."

Janice checked the light and adjusted her camera. Sally opened her sketch book, sharpened a pencil, and sat on the log, waiting. David had disappeared. Then, there were odd sounds like the snapping of twigs first from beyond the tree trunk.

"Look," said Florence, pointing. "What do we do?"

"Nothing," said Montana as a family of skunks marched around the fallen tree.

Janice aimed the camera and zoomed in on the leader of the skunks.

"How close can we get?" asked Sally hesitatingly.

Montana got on her hands and feet and slowly moved closer. "It's just me," she said so softly no one else heard her. "Follow me, Sally."

Sally stooped down and carefully got close to Montana. Janice stayed her distance, satisfied with the image she could get from her zoom lens. Oddly, the skunks sniffed around and edged their way closer to Montana.

While all this was going on, Dale could see David working the area at the top of the cliff. Moments later there was movement midway up the face of the cliff where limestone cropped out of the side. Then it disappeared.

The skunks suddenly stopped sniffing and moving, as if posing. Silence. Then they continued. Sally sketched as quickly as she could.

"I have it," she said.

Montana looked back at Janice and pointed to a sycamore tree only twenty feet away.

A bobcat had silently moved from the limestone cave to the tree and was now poised on a limb of the tree. At twenty feet its presence was threatening.

Montana just said, "Hey, kitty."

The bobcat glanced back to her and then to the skunks who were suddenly aware of its presence. Everyone looked back at the bobcat and when they turned to see the skunks, they were gone. The bobcat leaped to the forest floor and rushed to where the skunks had been. Montana motioned everyone to stay still. The cat then laid down and brushed its paw through the dirt. Now, on its side, it lay there as Sally frantically sketched its small face and slanted eyes.

"It's just a big kitty," she whispered, her pencil constantly moving.

"I know," whispered Montana.

Click. Click. The bobcat sniffed at the ground while Janice photographed the forest's pet cat.

"It's so perfect." Sally was actually sobbing. "Thank you," she said, looking somewhere to the top of the sycamore tree.

"Did you get them?" David whispered from behind them.

"It was amazing," said Dale.

"We got them," said Janice.

"That only took thirty minutes. You guys are good," said David. "Next stop, otters. Okay. Let's go."

He drove them to Bryan Park Road where the Grinnell Mill was and parked just off the road. He led them down the School Forest Trail to where it intersected Yellow Springs Creek.

"It's not far." They could tell they were getting close to the stream. The sound of water rushing over rocks got louder. David stopped and stepped off the path.

"You aren't supposed to leave the path. But this is for the pamphlet, so be careful. He led them to the bank of the creek and asked them to stay where they were and watch him. He looked around.

"Okay, come over here. Stand behind that log."

They obeyed.

"These are otter tracks. These are possum tracks. Here are deer tracks." As he said each one, he pointed out which were which in the mud. "Everybody comes here for a drink."

"Sit on the log there."

He had been carrying a net and dipped it in the stream, then stood still. He was like a statue, until he looked up at the Wesley Club and grinned. He moved the net through the water and pulled it above the stream and it seemed alive with the small fish. He laid the fish on the bank and then slapped the water with his hand a couple times and stepped away from the bank. The fish flopped around and just as it was about to rescue itself back into the creek, an otter swam up to it and grabbed it with its teeth, oblivious to the camera, the sketch book, and the kids sitting motionless on the log. Montana and David exchanged smiles. Sally sketched and sketched. Janice aimed her camera. *Click. Click.*

The Wesley Club was busy capturing the moment, but tears were in everyone's eyes as they watched the otter work on the fish and then a second otter, maybe the spouse, swam up and shared the bounty. As Janice and Sally went about the business of collecting images, Montana and the boys scoured this section of the Glen with their eyes.

"Follow this path toward that old oak," David said to Dale and Jesse. "Montana, you and William head to the Maple over there. Study the tree, each branch, especially the hollowed-out parts. Owls look like their surroundings, so you have to be looking for eyes, beaks, and talons."

"Listen," said Sally suddenly.

"What do you hear?" David asked.

"We heard it the other night when we found the beaver in the trap. Like a baby."

David's eyes moved from the tree line to the bank of the creek. "I hear it, too."

Montana moved up the stream toward the Maple tree but kept her eyes on the stream and the bank. She looked back at David and pointed. To her, it was unmistakable. It was the same size, had the same kind of leafy limbs on it. David walked over to her, nodded, put his finger to his lips for her to stay quiet. "Get Florence over here," he said. He scanned the entire area and abruptly turned his head away from the direction of the Grinnell Mill. Montana slowly went back to the girls and whispered to Florence. When she got to David, he said, "Watch the area directly behind me. What do you see?" There were plenty of trees, then there was a glint of light, a reflection of sun, like from a mirror or window, or binoculars.

"It's him," she said. "I know it."

Montana came back. "It's a beaver in that trap. We have to get it out. If the water gets higher it will drown."

"You're right," said David.

Sunday, May 18, 1958, 3:30 p.m.
Grinnell Mill Apartment

Vince leaned out the window of the old Mill and could see the Wesley Club was near his beaver trap.

"Who is that guy with those kids?" he said annoyingly.

"Where?" said Max.

Vince handed Max the binoculars. "Look through the trees close to the culvert up there then go a bit right.

"Hey, that's the girl that took our picture!"

"Yeah. They're getting too close to that trap."

“No, they’re moving on” Max spoke as he peered through the binoculars. “She must have gotten enough pictures. They’re all down by that big tree.”

“Let me see.” He took the binoculars back from Max.

Vince scanned the creek area. “I don’t see that guy. The kids are gawking at that tree. One kid’s drawing something. That girl you like is taking pictures. Wait, the boys are heading up the trail. The girls are following them.”

“Look,” said Max. It’s that guy that was with them. He’s coming down the road. And they both watched David, now carrying the beaver trap, walk to his truck, load the trap in the back of it, and drive up Corry Street toward the museum.

“That’s my trap!”

CHAPTER 14

Monday, May 19, 1958, 12:00 p.m.
Central Junior High School cafeteria

"We need to find the eagles," said Montana, poking at her mashed potatoes.

"Do you think the guy trapping the beaver took them?" asked Florence.

"Grandpa said there are people who pay for eagles. They either want them as kind of pets, like falcons, or to get their feathers. Poachers." She dropped her fork and gave up on eating.

"How are the eggs doing?" asked Sally.

"Okay. Grandpa talked to Mr. Atwell last night. He said his brooder is still sitting on them."

"When will they hatch?" asked Dale.

"The big question is if they hatch at all. Thirty-six days, but we don't know from when. Then we moved them so much that they may not hatch at all. We'll go from four eagles in Glen Helen to none." Montana buried her face in her hands.

"God will help us," said a small voice from under the table. Paddles gradually emerged from Florence's lap. "Dear God, please protect the eagles and the eagles' eggs. Help us to find them and return them safely to the forest. In Jesus' name, Amen."

"Amen," repeated the Wesley Club and a couple kids at the lunch tables nearby.

"What would poachers around here do with eagles?" asked William. "Sell them?"

"Who would they sell them to?"

The room suddenly got darker.

"Somebody just turned the lights out," said Dale.

They watched the kitchen staff come out of the kitchen and check the switches, but nothing would turn the lights back on. Kids moved their trays to the tables close to the windows. The principal walked in and conferred with a couple teachers. Gradually, the rest of the students in the school were directed into the cafeteria. Then the school custodian came in, his shirt soaked with water.

"We have an announcement to make," began the principal. "We have a water line broken on the second floor and it has caused all the power to this building to be disrupted. I'm afraid we will have to cancel the rest of today."

Before he finished his comments, whoops and hollers filled the room. He smiled and held up his hands for quiet.

"Listen on the radio for updates regarding tomorrow's classes. Teachers will be posted in the hallways with flashlights so you can get your things out of your lockers. You are dismissed."

"What will we do?" Sally said.

"Wait here," said Florence. "Who has a nickel? I'll call Aunt Audrey." Dale handed her a coin.

After fifteen minutes, Florence came back.

"They need more pay phones here. Everyone was making calls. We can go to Mr. Gregory's office as long as we don't make a ruckus."

They dispersed to their bikes after securing their books.

Monday, May 19, 1958, 12:30 p.m.
Ye Olde Trail Inn Tavern, Yellow Springs

"Good afternoon, Baron," the woman said.

"How's my birds, Fraulein?"

"*Our* birds, Liebchen. Good news. We are all set for Wednesday night. We have six buyers."

"Our birds. How are they?"

"I have to keep them covered. The male is not eating. I may have to force feed him."

"Where are they?"

"Didn't you know? Your boys are keeping them in the basement of that Mill."

"Do you trust them?"

"I told them you'd give them a bonus. Max is staying with the birds while Vince gets you that other beaver. And I check on them each day."

Monday, May 19, 1958, 12:30 p.m.
Mr. Gregory's Law Office

"Can we use the conference room?" asked Florence when she arrived at Mr. Gregory's law office.

"What's up?" asked her aunt Audrey.

"The eagles. We're going to find out who poached them." Suddenly the door to the conference room opened and Mr. Wells, Mr. Gregory, and Florence's mother and dad walked out, all smiles.

"Honey, what are you doing here?" said Rachel Williams.

"No school. A water pipe busted."

"Burst, dear. Good news, we are moving this weekend. The house is ours, thanks to Mr. Gregory and Mr. Wells."

Florence hugged her mom just as Sally and Jesse walked in the office.

"What's going on?" asked Mr. Gregory.

"Someone poached our eagles," said Montana as she walked in the office. "We're going to track them down."

"They want to use the conference room," said Audrey.

"Are we finished?" he asked.

"You are. No more appointments. I can file those at the courthouse if they're all signed," she said.

"You'll clean up after yourselves, right?" he said.

"Yes, sir."

"Here, Florence, you may want to get some Cokes. The big ones." He handed her five dollars. "Two six packs."

"Dale, we need Janice and the photos," said Montana.

Dale looked at Audrey and she pointed to the phone at her desk.

"I'll be back in thirty minutes," Audrey said as she thumbed through the papers Mr. Gregory just handed her. "Florence, you guys will need pencils and a legal pad."

"And the wall, okay?" Florence asked. They all looked at the plain wall next to the conference table, peppered with tacks, scotch tape residue, and nails where once a picture or two was hung.

"The tape's on the table there," said Audrey.

By now everyone in the Wesley Club was setting books on the table. Sally thumbed through her sketch pad for sheets of paper with lists they had made that weekend about the clues they had about the missing eagles.

"Any word on the eagles?" William asked as Montana came into the conference room.

"Grandpa said they are not there. He's hoping we can finish up the pamphlet if there's no school."

"We can plan it here first. What's left?" said William.

"Right. Not much after our hike with David. Sally, do you have the list?" said Montana.

"Here it is. Oh, look. Isn't he beautiful?" She opened her book to the great horned owl she had sketched.

"David knows all those animals. It's like he's their shepherd," said Montana.

"Mr. Doolittle," Jesse said as Florence walked in with cold Cokes. Dale helped her put one pack in the refrigerator.

"Are they really dating?" Montana asked Florence under her breath.

"Aunt Audrey? David? They go out in the evening to give me and my parents time alone," said Florence.

"I want a David," said Montana blushing.

"Mr. and Mrs. Doolittle," said Jesse. Montana shot him a mean look.

"Rabbit, fox, and goose," said Sally.

"That's all? I can't believe we haven't gotten a rabbit yet," said Montana.

CHAPTER 15

Monday, May 19, 1958, 2:15 p.m.
Grinnell Mill Apartment

"Vince, why does he need another beaver? Isn't one enough to build a dam?" Max and Vince sat together at the table, watching the lonely beaver lay on his side.

"He needs a girlfriend, you know, a family, so they can take care of the dam."

"He needs a reason to stay. What's to keep him from going back to the stream?"

"That's what I said, you idiot!" Vince snapped at Max and looked out the window. "I have to get another beaver. You stay here while I scout around. You haven't seen that guy's truck, have you?"

"No," Max responded. He kept studying the beaver. "That's a fine pelt."

Monday, May 19, 1958, 1:30 p.m.
Mr. Gregory's Law Office

Audrey Thorne walked into the office and looked at the progress the Wesley Club had achieved. One sheet of paper had the word PAMPHLET on top, followed by:

Fox

Rabbit

Goose

All written in a column. Another sheet of paper had a much longer list:

CLUES

Footprint at nest

Rusty Climber

Beaver Trap

Robertson Screw

Canadian License

Glow

Photo inside Canadian truck

Sketch of Man #1

Sketch of Eagles

There was another list:

PLACES

Eagle Nest

YS Creek

Museum Parking Lot

South YS Creek.

"You have been busy. I understand the 'pamphlet.'"

"You wouldn't know where David is, Miss Thorne? We need his help finding three more animals," said Montana.

"He's in his office I think." She went to her desk, picked up the phone and dialed a number from heart.

"Is Mr. Brown there?" she asked, holding the phone to her ear. "Mr. Brown? Hold on please, I have a Miss Montana MacCarthy for you, person to person," and handed the phone to Montana, who held it to her ear wide eyed and silent.

"Hello?" could be heard repeated on the other end. Then she got her composure.

"David. This is Montana. We need your help. We need a fox, a goose, and a rabbit."

"You don't have a rabbit?" he asked.

"I know. It just slipped by us."

"They're everywhere."

"I know. Can you help?" She was nearly in tears.

"Yes, when do you need it?"

"Grandpa wants to finish the brochure on Wednesday." She fiddled with the phone's cord as she spoke.

"Are you at Mr. Gregory's or Audrey's?"

"Mr. Gregory's."

"What are you doing now?"

"We're studying clues," she said, scanning the room. "We have to find those eagles."

"Why don't you leave that to me?"

Montana paused for a brief moment. "Do you know where they are?"

"No. But I have a couple leads. Why aren't you guys in school?"

"A pipe burst. They had to close the school."

"Okay. I'll be at the fish hatchery tomorrow. Can you guys meet me there after school?"

"I don't think there will be school."

"I'll be there all day. Come at ten if there's no school. You'll get your rabbit for sure."

"What about the goose?"

"Have you ever heard of Shawnee Park?"

Montana hit her head with her hand and looked into the conference room as the kids were working on the list.

Montana repeated the information to Sally and Janice, who was pulling photos out of an envelope. They agreed to the plan, and she repeated the information to David and handed the phone back to Audrey.

"Pray for no school," she said as she walked back in the room. "Janice and Sally, we have to go to the park."

"Why?"

"Goose."

"We'll be back in a half hour," said Montana. The three girls walked out together.

Monday, May 19, 1958, 3:15 p.m.
Shawnee Park, Xenia

Montana, Sally, and Janice walked the three blocks to Shawnee Park and even from a half block away they spied two geese swimming in the pond.

"I feel so stupid," muttered Montana, nearly in tears.

"Why?" asked Janice.

"David knew that I should know where to find geese."

"That's okay, we all knew there were geese here. We didn't know where we could find geese at the Glen. That's all. It's no big thing," said Janice.

"Yes, it is."

Sally went to the edge of the pond, and as usual, the geese and ducks swam toward her, begging for a morsel of bread, or cracker, or some other food you were not allowed to feed to the animals in Shawnee Park. The sun poked through the trees and Sally used the rays as light on her sketch pad. She sat, drawing, studying the geese, and effectively captured the ripples the birds made in the pond.

Click. Click. The geese continued their swim, still hoping one of the girls would slip them a snack. Finally, one of the geese swam to the very bank of the pond and with a flap of her wings and a quick step of her feet climbed up on the bank and made a bee line for Sally. Montana moved close to the bird and tenderly picked it up and held it where Sally could finish the details of the feathers on its neck.

Click. Janice got the close up.

"This is so easy," she said.

"Guess what?" Montana whispered.

"What?" said Sally.

"There is a bunny rabbit just behind you." Montana gingerly put the goose down on the ground and shooed it into the pond. "Are you finished with that one?"

"I guess so," said Sally.

"Don't move. I'll get this little guy ready." She eased her way behind Sally and sat down beside the rabbit.

"Turn around. He's ready." Sally started sketching. *Click. Click.* Janice got the rabbit, doing all she could to keep Montana out of the view. A robin landed next to Montana and just looked up at her. *Hoot. Hoot.* An owl made its presence known from the fork of the maple tree it sat in.

"Who needs David?" said Janice chuckling. "All you have to do is stand there. Do we have that one?"

"No, it's a Saw Whet."

"Look how little it is!"

"I love the yellow eyes." *Click. Click.*

"How long do you need, Sally?"

"A couple more minutes. I could stay here all day." She continued to sketch while Montana and Janice contentedly sat.

Activity at a park bench in front of the park pavilion caught Montana's eye. A man and a woman were studying a sheet of paper with a list on it. When the woman turned it over, photos of two eagles were visible. Montana's heart skipped a beat.

"Look, Janice, Sally, do you know those people?"

Janice was the first to look and then suddenly turned her back to them.

"Sally don't look at them. That's the guy in the car by the museum the other day."

"They have a flier with pictures of two eagles!" Montana said.

"Are they your eagles?" asked Janice.

"I have to get closer." She stood up and began making her way over to them.

"Use your powers Miss Doolittle," Sally said still looking down at her sketch pad. She and Janice giggled.

Montana started walking toward the couple at the picnic table, with a Robin perched on her shoulder and the little Saw Whet owl in her hand. She just wanted to get close enough to get a better look at the eagle photos.

"Well, young lady. You seem to have a way with birds," said Fraulein Schmidt.

Montana took a deep breath, "I think they like me. Would you like to hold one?" She walked closer.

The man and the woman looked surprised, and the woman set the paper down on the table, list side up as Montana handed her the Saw Whet now perched on her finger. The woman could not resist.

"Is this a pet?" she asked.

"Oh, no. They live here in the park." Montana glanced at the paper to see nothing but names of men and cities. She needed to see the other side. As if the robin read her mind, he flew up, then down toward the paper causing the Saw Whet to take flight, both birds fanning the paper enough to blow it off the table.

"Oh. Sorry. Sorry." The paper landed on the grass, eagle side up. Montana's heart leapt. They were her eagles, there was a date and a place listed and she memorized it all as she lifted the paper from the ground and placed it back on the table, list side up.

"They get nervous sometimes. Are you okay?"

"We're fine. Very impressive, young lady."

Montana needed to get away before she forgot the details on the other side of the flier.

"Can you get them back?"

"Probably not, ma'am. Once they're frightened, they go hide some place."

"Sit down, child," said the Baron. Montana sat down with them, trying to remain calm.

"Where did you learn this? Handling animals like that?" the woman asked.

"Grandpa says I was born with it." Montana kept repeating the phone number to herself so she would not forget.

"Do you ever handle eagles?" she asked. "Like these?" The Baron cleared his throat. Montana got one more look at the details.

"I'd love to handle an eagle. There aren't any around here," she said quickly, afraid to blow her cover. Then she got up.

"It was good to meet you."

"What's your name girl?" the Baron asked.

Montana thought quickly. "Erin. I'm Irish."

"Oh my. I guess you are. Goodbye Erin." They looked back down at the paper having no idea who they had actually been talking to.

Montana continued her walk away from the picnic table, away from Sally and Janice and followed the path that led completely around the pavilion. She watched from her peripheral vision as the man and woman also left. Then she watched them get into the BMW roadster. She waited for it to pull out of the parking spot before she headed back to Sally and Janice.

"That was them!" said Janice.

"Look," Sally turned in her sketch pad for the drawing of the man in the back seat of the carry all. "Here, I drew her while you were talking." She showed Montana a full-page sketch of the woman at the picnic table.

"What a good idea, Sally!"

"I was so scared. Here, write this down: Wednesday, May 21. Whiteflower Farm. 7 pm. Auction. Phone number 555-3343. Oh, write this down: GB678335. That's the guy's license. We found my eagles! They're okay!"

Sally rapidly scribbled her words and the three left the park, watching to be sure they weren't being followed.

CHAPTER 16

Monday, May 19, 1958, 4:00 p.m.
Mr. Gregory's Law Office

"What about the climbers?" asked William.

"They were rusty, like they were used."

"They were old alright," said Florence. "The leather strap was brittle and old."

"Antique store?" asked Dale. "Maybe we can check with them."

William wrote that down beside *climbers*.

Just then Montana, Sally, and Janice walked in.

"We found the eagles," said Montana. She looked over to Audrey. "Can David come over here?"

Audrey picked up the phone and called.

"What? Where?" asked Jesse.

Just then, Mr. Gregory walked out of his office.

"How's it going, kids?"

"Montana says they found the eagles. Where'd you guys go?" asked Audrey.

"To the park. We were photographing a goose and rabbit." Montana described in detail all that happened while Mr. Gregory took a seat at the conference table. Sally drew out the description of the flier as Montana described it. Two eagle photos, the word 'auction,' Whiteflower Farm, May 21, 7 p.m.

"They got in a sports car. BMW. License?" Montana looked over at Sally.

"GB678335," said Sally on cue and wrote down the number on her depiction of the flier.

Mr. Gregory stared at the wall with lists of clues and the image of the flier, including the sketch of the eagles.

"Audrey, come here." She walked in with her notepad and instinctively handed him a yellow legal pad.

"First of all, is there some kind of crime here?" he asked.

"Somebody poached two eagles from Glen Helen," said Montana, defensively.

"Is poaching illegal?"

"Yes," said a voice from the entry.

"Hi, David. That was quick," said Audrey.

"What?"

"I just tried to call you. They said you were out," she said.

"Somebody is trying to sell off two eagles in Yellow Springs. We just got a tip."

Mr. Gregory pointed to the sketch of the flier.

"You're kidding." David studied it for a minute. "What's this?"

"You told us to go to the park to get the goose. Guess who was there?" said Montana.

"These guys." Sally taped the drawing of the Baron and the woman next to the flier.

"They had this flier and I got to peek at it with the help of a robin and a Saw Whet owl."

"You talked to these people? Are you kidding?" David looked around the room Mr. Gregory shrugged his shoulders. "It's what they do."

"What?" said David.

"Solve crimes."

"We haven't solved it yet. They still have my eagles," said Montana.

Mr. Gregory pulled a chair out for David to sit down. "Who saw these two steal the eagles?"

"No one."

"No witnesses?"

"They probably didn't do it. I bet they paid those guys in the old car."

"What guys?" asked Mr. Gregory.

"These guys." Sally pulled out another sketch and Janice pulled out a photograph from her envelope and then taped them beside the sketch of the man and woman at the park.

"Oh, and this guy," Montana pointed at the man from the park. "The woman called him Baron."

"What do you think?" Mr. Gregory asked David.

"The Whiteflower Farm was just sold or rented, the last I knew." He was looking at the flier.

"Are we sure these are your eagles?" asked Mr. Gregory.

"Yes, sir. These are my eagles," said Montana.

"You mean the Glen's eagles," said David.

"Same thing." She blushed. "I just know God wants me to protect them. They trust me."

He didn't challenge her.

"Is there a crime here, David?"

"So far, yes. We just don't have any witnesses."

"We saw this guy try to trap a beaver. Montana got it loose," said Dale pointing at the photo of Vince Arledge.

Janice pulled out the picture of the trap and tacked it on the wall.

"Attempted poaching," said David.

"The eagles have to be there." Montana pointed at the flier about the auction at the Whiteflower farm.

"We have a crime. We have evidence. We have suspects," said Audrey.

"Who do we call, David?"

"Wildlife and Fisheries. That's me. But I think we'll need the Sheriff. This place is not in the city."

One by one the kids noticed that David's uniform had patches that said U.S. Wildlife and Fisheries. He was no longer their guide in Glen Helen, a Sunday school teacher, or the almost boyfriend of Florence's aunt.

"Do you have a gun?" asked William.

"Hopefully we won't need weapons, William. But yes. I do."

"Wow," said a couple of the kids, including Montana.

David sat in the chair and stared at the wall riddled with clues.

"What are you thinking, David?"

"Are they hiding the eagles at the Whiteflower Farm? That wouldn't be smart. How many barns are in Glen Helen? Not all the land is set aside with trails. Maybe some area they have not gotten to."

"Do you have any aerial views?"

"Let's check with your grandpa, Montana, and his group."

"Bad news, kids. I just heard on the radio, no school tomorrow," said Audrey from her desk.

"Aww. No. How disappointing," said Florence with a huge smile on her face.

"Okay, meet me at the museum tomorrow at nine in the morning. Let's find that fox," said David. "Is that soon enough to finish your pamphlet?" David looked at Janice.

"I have classes tomorrow, but Dale can take the pictures. I'll meet you all at the museum tomorrow at noon," she said.

"Okay everyone. Shawnee Park tomorrow morning," said Sally. "We'll leave together."

Tuesday, May 20, 1958, 8:00 a.m.
Shawnee Park

The Wesley Club met on their bikes at the pavilion of Shawnee Park.

"We have to hurry to get there by nine," said Jesse.

"Do we go up 68?" asked Dale.

"No, Kinsey Road, and then we go out Stevenson Road. I nearly got killed once going out 68," said Montana.

"Let's go," said William. Each kid had a canteen full of water and snacks and a jacket in the bicycle basket or saddle bags. Montana led the group through back streets and across vacant lots until they got to Kinsey Road.

They were five minutes late getting to the museum, but David was there waiting for them. They parked their bikes in the racks.

"Okay, we're going to the horse farm. Is a fox all we are after?"

"That's it," said Montana.

"We'll be heading upriver once we get there."

They got into the back of David's truck and bounced most of the way over the farm road leading to the farm. They stopped and walked a few hundred yards through a meadow and then into the Glen area, thick with trees, many were sycamores with white bark. David started following an animal path abundant with deer, raccoon, and rabbit tracks.

"Here." He stopped and stepped away from the path to let the six kids bunch up close to him. "Fox," he said. He pointed down at the track.

"It looks like a dog track," said Montana.

"It's a red fox, I'm pretty sure. It's fresh so you guys follow about twenty feet behind me. Hold them here, Montana, then start. Try to stay off the path."

It took ten minutes for David to find the source of the tracks. He stopped walking and gradually crouched down close to the shrubs and bushes. He motioned to Montana, and she crouched, but continued with the club to just behind David. She motioned Sally and Dale to the front, along the path. There, before them, was the red fox.

"It's skinny," whispered William, eyes locked on the creature.

Sally sketched while Dale adjusted the camera.

"Dale, hold off for a few minutes. Let Sally get her drawing first," said David. They watched the fox licking at a fallen nest where eggshells were broken, quite visible to the club.

They watched Sally develop the face, body, and fur, and then fill in areas she had sketched just a couple lines. And then the tail, which completed the basic drawing.

"I'm done," said Sally. "Take your pictures."

Click. Click. The fox's head jerked up and she looked around before returning to her meal, and Sally studied her drawing. *Click*. Dale took one more shot, and the fox fled immediately, heading up the Little Miami River.

"He's heading back to his den," said David. "Did you get what you need?"

"Yes, sir," said Dale.

"I just have a few finishing touches." The rest of the club agreed that the fox Sally had sketched was perfect. David led them back to his truck.

Tuesday, May 20, 1958, 11:00 a.m.
Atwell Turkey Farm

Mr. Atwell walked the length of the turkey hatchery to check on the brooder he had assigned to the eagle eggs. Oddly, nothing was sitting on the eggs. He touched them and felt the warmness, looked around the building and was startled when the brooder gobbled and hopped into the nest.

"Ah. I caught you on a break didn't I." The brooder turkey nestled in, contented with her assignment.

Tuesday, May 20, 1958, 12:30 p.m.
Trailside Museum

"Free at last!" exclaimed Janice once she walked through the museum doors. "Did you get the fox?" she asked.

Dale handed her the camera and Sally handed her the sketch.

"He's beautiful," she said.

"David says he's a she," said William. "We have everything laid out."

"I'm thinkin' that fox would be the cover," Mr. MacCarthy said. Then Sally handed him a sheet of paper.

"Oh my," he said. Sally had created a composite of the fox, raccoon, horned owl, skunk, bobcat, and eagle posed on or under a single oak tree.

"I like this," he said and handed it to Janice who smiled and winked at Sally. The two of them left for the dark room where the other pages were laid out on the table. After discussing sizes and number of pages and how to staple it all together, Mr. MacCarthy left her and Dale to finish the photography just as a deluge of rain pelted the roof and the skies went dark as night.

"This is not going to be fun going home," said Jesse as he stared out the window.

"Good news, kids," said Mrs. MacCarthy. "No school. You're done for the year according to the radio."

"What? Are you sure?" asked Jesse. "Wait until Dale hears this."

"How do we know if we passed?" asked Sally.

"They will post all the kids that passed at the library tomorrow. It said if you're not on the passed list, then check the summer school list."

"So, we meet at the library tomorrow?" asked Jesse.

"At ten, okay?" said Sally.

Then, Dale walked out of the dark room and slumped into a chair by the door.

"Are you alright? What's wrong?"

"My settings were all off. We couldn't get the first picture to develop. They were too dark. Not enough light."

"Well, let's see what we have." Mr. MacCarthy went back into the dark room followed by the Wesley Club, all except Dale.

"I'm sorry, Mr. MacCarthy. We lost the fox," said Janice.

A sudden clap of thunder jolted the building.

"Do you remember where the tracks were?" Jesse whispered to Montana.

"I think so, but we won't find a fox in this weather," she whispered back.

"The director comes tomorrow at four to approve the layout. I have a file cabinet full of some photos. I just don't recall if we have a fox." He walked out of the dark room and into the office.

When Janice and Dale finished measuring the layout, they all shuffled through hundreds of photographs looking for a fox.

"Dale, good news. No more school this year. They can't fix that leak in time."

"How do I know if I passed?" he asked.

"They'll have a list posted at the library tomorrow. We should all meet there," said Jesse. Dale continued to sit in the chair.

"I think we can work with just the fox drawing," said Mr. MacCarthy after they all had scanned the photos from the file cabinet. "It's so odd. Not one fox photo." He left the room.

Dale stared at the wall.

"We'll try again tomorrow, okay, Dale?" said Montana. "Grandpa would really like to get a fox on the cover."

Dale lit up. "I know I can get a better shot. I know what I did wrong. Do you think we can find that fox again?"

"I know I can." She turned to the others. "One more trip, first thing in the morning, okay?"

After half an hour, the rain let up.

"I have to get home," said Jesse. He and Dale looked outside. The rain had become a drizzle.

"I'll take your bikes to the church," said Mr. MacCarthy.

"Or the library, just in case they get the list up early," Jesse said.

Dale nodded, "Yes!"

"Jesse, William, and Sally, you guys come with me. Janice, can you take Dale and Florence? I'll take the bikes in the truck."

Once they were in Mr. MacCarthy's truck, William spoke up.

"Dale's worried he isn't going to pass this year."

"Really? Wouldn't we know if he was in trouble with his grades?" said Sally.

"We're in English together," said William. "He's good in class but he gets his homework in late."

"We're in Science together. He's fine there. He gets As and Bs," said Jesse.

"Same in Math," said Sally. "I think he worries too much. I bet his grades are just fine."

"I hated English. Of course, I was in Scotland when I took it. But Gaelic? I didn't like that either," said Mr. MacCarthy and they all laughed. "Ah, here, let's take a little detour." He turned left off Rt. 68 to Hyde Road.

"I'm takin' it slow. Watch around the farm buildings as I drive down this lane."

And just then he turned down a gravel lane and slowed as he got to the large two-story white brick farmhouse.

"Let's see if that sports car is here." He followed down the lane past the house to the barn.

"Do you see anything?"

"Nothing here," said William.

"It looks vacant," said Sally.

He turned his truck around at the gate leading out to the pasture and drove slowly past the large manor house.

"Did you see the man by the creek?" said Sally.

"I did. We're just goin' to keep drivin'."

"It's such a big farm."

"Two hundred acres, I hear."

"What was beside the man? A box?" asked William.

"It looked like a cage," said Mr. MacCarthy.

"By the way, that's where the Baron lives that Montana was talking about."

He continued up the lane back to Hyde Road and proceeded on to Xenia.

Dale and Florence were waiting there for their bikes.

"We drove by the Baron's house," said Jesse.

"What's it like?" asked Florence.

"Big," said Sally.

"Are the lists up?" asked William.

"We haven't checked," said Florence.

"Let's go then." They walked their bikes to the rack and started up the steps.

Jesse was the first to go inside with Sally. They held the door open, but William, Florence, and Dale were in deep conversation. "C'mon, let's check for him."

When Jesse and Sally got to the bulletin board, there was no list.

"Mrs. MacCarthy said they'd post it tomorrow," said Sally.

"Right. Okay. I have to get home to take over babysitting Christina."

"Tomorrow at eight, Jesse," said Sally. She reached out for his hand, and he reached back with a smile for the joy of her touch that tingled up his arm.

"Tomorrow," he said.

CHAPTER 17

Wednesday, May 21, 1958, 8 a.m.
Shawnee Park

Bike by bike, the Wesley Club met at Shawnee Park with the intention of accomplishing two things: finish the Glen Helen pamphlet and recover the eagles they were sure were poached from the nest in the large oak at the base of the 100 steps leading to the Glen trails.

"Montana, what are you doing here?" asked Sally.

"I'm going with you guys. Grandpa has a meeting in Dayton and will meet us at the museum later. We can go straight from here to where I think we'll get the fox."

"Where's that?" asked Dale. There was a large camera bag in the bicycle basket.

"The old Mill. Close to where David took us."

"Can we check the library first?"

"Not if you want a photo of the fox in the pamphlet. Today's our last chance and that fox doesn't go out during the day. Grandpa won't be too happy," said Montana.

Dale looked so sad. It was very clear he could not function until he was sure he had passed.

"Maybe my sketch would be enough," said Sally.

"Grandpa really wants the photo of the fox on the cover. Photo on the front and your sketch on the back. I mean. Well. We have a deadline. Dale, maybe we can call the library and ask." Montana was convincing as to the importance.

"Maybe we could take the pictures," said William.

"I can't let this camera out of my sight or hands. Janice will kill me."

The Wesley Club all looked at each other, except Dale. "Maybe they posted it on the window. Go ahead. I'll catch up with you." He started pedaling toward the library.

"It's just a few minutes," said Florence. She followed him.

"That fox is not going to wait," yelled Montana after them. William followed Florence.

"Maybe the fox will cooperate," said Sally, and that was enough to send the last three of the club directly behind Dale.

Dale was already up the steps of the library when Sally and Jesse hopped off their bikes to join the club. But Dale just sat down on the steps.

"Bad news?" asked William.

"No news," said Florence.

"Wait," said Jesse. "I thought about this and here's what we need to do. Florence and I really don't have anything else to do with the pamphlet. We'll stay here and wait for the library to open. You guys go ahead. We'll call the museum as soon as the library opens and the post the grades."

"That's a long wait," said Sally.

"It'll work. We'll go to Mr. Gregory's office while we're waiting. We can help Aunt Audrey," said Florence.

"You guys call as soon as you check the list. Okay?" yelled Dale as he pedaled his bike with Montana, William, and Sally.

"Check everybody's name," yelled William.

"What's he worried about?" said Florence. "He's the smartest kid in the school."

"I know. What are we going to do while we're waiting for the library to open?"

"Audrey will think of something."

Wednesday, May 21, 1958, 8:40 a.m.
Stevenson Road Covered Bridge

After five minutes of cycling through driving rain and moments of deafening thunder, Montana was the first to lean her bike against the wall of the covered bridge on Stevenson Road. One by one William, Sally, and Dale lined up behind her, each one leaning close to the wall to allow any cars easy passage through the one lane bridge.

"Grandpa is going to kill me. We're not going to find a fox with this kind of rain and it's going to be too late."

"I'm sorry. This is all my fault," said Dale. "My dad told me that if my grades weren't improved, I won't be able to go to Philmont." He wiped the rain off the camera case with his shirt.

"Where's Paddles when you need her?" asked Sally.

"What?" said Montana.

A clap of thunder jolted the entire bridge.

"Okay. God's close by. God, hear our prayer. Philmont is important to Dale, and we ask that you work his grades so his dad will let him go. And, God, that fox. Help us to find that fox. We don't want to hurt him. We just want to make him famous. We love you God. Oh, please, keep

Jesse and Florence safe. And, let them be bearers of good news. Amen."

Rumbles of thunder seemed to respond to Sally's prayer.

"I hope He got all that," Sally said.

"He gets everything," said William.

In moments the rumbles sounded further away and then the clouds broke, and the sun shone through the spaces between the wooden boards protecting the Stevenson Road bridge.

"Let's get that fox," yelled Montana as they sped out of the bridge, into sunlight, and toward the Grinnell Mill and their elusive fox.

Wednesday, May 21, 1958, 9:20 a.m.
Grinnell Mill

Vince Aldridge pulled into the gravel driveway by the Grinnell Mill apartment. He was carrying one of his brown canvas bags and lay it beside the couch where Max was dozing.

"Oh Max. Oh Max! Look what I have."

Max squinted, then reached for the back of the couch and pulled himself up, now face to face with a brown bag whining and sitting on the coffee table.

"Mrs. Beaver?" he said with a groggy voice.

"Mrs. Beaver. Did you ever doubt me? The best trapper in Canada. Now, the best trapper in the U.S. We're set now, Max. Wait until that Baron gets a load of this. Keep her here while I build a cage."

Vince opened the back window and let a long extension cord drop the one story to the picnic table set out back. He then took a couple lengths of 1" x 2" pine boards outside and cut them the width of the roll of chicken wire that was already stored under the table. It took only a few minutes for him to screw the boards together in the form of a box. He went back around the building and into their apartment.

"Max, come here. Look." He was looking out the back window with his binoculars. "Do you know them? Is that the girl that was taking pictures?"

"Let me see." After heaving himself off the couch, he took the binoculars and studied hard. "It's just four kids. The photographer girl was blond. This gal's a redhead."

"The other one's a blond. Look, there's four of them."

CHAPTER 18

Wednesday, May 21, 1958, 9:20 a.m.
Grinnell Mill Bridge

Montana stopped just before the Grinnell Road bridge over the Little Miami River.

"We follow that animal path." She pointed to the right side of the road. "We'll put our bikes behind that bush over there."

"What's that?" William was looking at a three-story building just off Grinnell Road.

"That's the mill. We found the barred owl and otters on the other side of it in the creek."

He studied the surroundings. "Oh, yeah."

They lifted the bikes over the railing and laid them in the grass behind a large hydrangea bush.

By now, the Wesley Club was familiar with animal paths and the signs small animals left, including tracks, marks on bark, feeding leftovers, and even their skat, or poop. Raccoon tracks were everywhere.

"What's this?" asked Dale, ready to snap a picture.

"Bunny rabbit tracks," said Montana.

Wednesday, May 21, 1958, 9:55 a.m.
Xenia Library

Jesse and Florence showed up five minutes before the library opened. There were others waiting, including the assistant principal for Central Junior High School.

"Hi, Mrs. Powers," said Jesse.

"Hello, Jesse. I bet you guys are happy about the early summer vacation."

"You bet. We want to check to make sure we passed."

"You're Florence, right?" she asked, now facing her.

"Yes ma'am. We need to check for our friends, too."

"I have everything here." She opened a folder. "We didn't do the names alphabetical. But I know you two passed. Give me the names of..."

"Dale Pyle, did he pass?" Florence jumped right to the mission.

"Oh, yes, I already know he passed, who's next?"

They gave her Montana, William, and Sally's names. "They all passed. Tell William that he will be in honors classes. Oh, and you, too, Florence." Suddenly, Florence stood a little taller. Jesse gave her a sideways glance and could tell she was beaming from the news.

"Thanks, Mrs. Powers," Jesse and Florence said almost at the same time and just as the library opened.

"We can call from here," said Jesse. They went up to the pay phone, dropped a nickel in and dialed the number to the museum.

"Hello, Mrs. MacCarthy? Yes, ma'am, it's Jesse. Is Dale Pyle there? ... Not yet? They were going to get pictures of a fox. ... Yes. We're just leaving. Florence and I are on our bikes. Yes, ma'am. Tell Dale he passed. Tell everyone they passed. Okay, yes, Montana, too."

Wednesday, May 21, 1958, 10:00 a.m.
Grinnell Mill Woods

"Look. This is fox," Montana whispered while pointing to tracks by the water. "Little guy got a drink here." She motioned them to stoop down, each one looking around to get a glimpse of their last animal for the pamphlet.

William suddenly grabbed Montana's arm. "Snake," he said, in a surprisingly quiet tone, but his grip was firm.

"Oh, don't worry. It's a water snake. They're harmless."

"It's still a snake." His eyes were fixed on the reptile.

"Shh. Look." She pointed in the water at four or five other snakes moving together. Suddenly the other kids were becoming less afraid and more fascinated by their antics in the water.

"Hmm. Little bunnies, hungry fox," Montana said, pointing to very tiny tracks on the path. "Follow me."

She led them a few yards off the path where she had seen the tracks. "Over there, in the tall grass. Look carefully." She backed them away a few feet. "See it?"

"I do," said Dale, aiming his camera.

"Me, too. I have to get closer," said Sally.

"Crouch down like this. Follow me, slowly," said Montana.

After a few feet Sally decided she was close enough and started sketching. The fox glanced at Sally, then Montana, then just stood there, as two fox kits played their way to her, jumping on each other. Montana looked at them and they looked at her, still keeping a distance of four yards.

"I don't know how you do it," said Sally, continuing her sketching, now including two kit faces in the image.

"Sally, you don't know how much I want to be able to sketch them like you."

"I didn't know that. I'll show you."

Click. Dale adjusted the settings more than once, clicking pictures after each adjustment. He took two more pictures but slipped on the dewy grass bank he was standing on. Instantly, the foxes darted off.

"Sorry," he said with a groan.

"I'm good," said Sally as Dale and Montana admired the pencil sketch of the mother fox and two kits with part of the stream in the background. "I'll finish the stream back at the museum."

Wednesday, May 21, 1958, 10:30 a.m.
Stevenson Road Covered Bridge

"I thought you said this was a short cut," Florence said as they walked their bikes through a muddy path at the edge of the golf course.

"Let's go over there. There's a golf cart path. Nobody's out here yet."

"There's a house," Florence said, pointing at a home with yellow shutters.

"Good. No fence. Let's cut between those houses."

Once the pair got to the street they got back on their bikes and raced down toward Kinsey Road, mud spinning off their wheels. A mist was hugging the road. As they looked out on the farmland, fields were already showing evidence of corn and soybean plants.

"Can we stop?" Florence asked, once they reached the Stevenson Road covered bridge. "You don't have any water, do you?" she asked.

He pulled a canteen out of his saddle bag on the bike.

"Do you want to split a Baby Ruth?" He asked, thinking she might be hungry, too. He broke the candy bar in half and then opened the package.

"Yum." She looked up at Jesse, then rolled her eyes. "Look beside your head. I swear you and Sally are ridiculous."

He turned his head to see a folded-up piece of paper with his name written on it neatly slipped in between a bridge joist and one of the boards protecting the bridge from rain and other elements.

"She says they are going to the old Grinnell Mill to find a fox."

"Is that all?" she said teasingly.

"Yep," he said, slightly disappointed. He looked at his watch. "We're two hours behind them."

“Montana would have found a fox within two hours, right?”

“I know. It’s on the way, so we’ll check it out. If we don’t see their bikes, we go on to the museum.”

CHAPTER 19

Wednesday, May 21, 1958, 10:30 a.m.
Mr. Gregory's Office

Mr. Gregory stared at the wall in his conference room, now riddled with sketches, photos, and lists of clues and places.

"David's here, Mr. Gregory."

"Send him in."

"Have you studied these?" asked Mr. Gregory when David walked in.

"Not exactly, but these kids have a similar set at the Trailside Museum in Glen Helen."

"It's like they are one mind in individual bodies," Mr. Gregory said, shaking his head.

"This one interests me." David went to the sketch Sally did of the flier Montana saw on the picnic table.

"These people have to be stupid. Using fliers to announce an illegal auction," said Mr. Gregory.

"Our problem is we have to catch them with the goods. You know, in the act. For example, if we show up at this barn, they'll just let the animals loose and deny they had anything to do with these handwritten fliers. The eagles will fly away, and they'll get away Scot free."

"So, you have to get them with the birds." Mr. Gregory now looked directly at David.

"We have to get them in the act of selling them and then we have a maximum sentence we can impose on them. That's why I came to see you."

David shut the door to the conference room.

Wednesday, May 21, 1958, 10:45 a.m.
Whiteflower Farm

"Okay, how much will we get out of this auction, Fraulein?" asked the Baron as he looked out over the area of his farm that was to become a pond.

"You get $1,000 each. I get the rest. That's our deal."

The phone rang.

"It's for you. He's asking about the auction." He handed the phone to Fraulein Schmidt.

"What? Yes. Seven o'clock. No. How do you know this? Where did you get this number?" She looked worried, cupped her hand over the mouthpiece of the phone.

"Look out the window, Liebchen. See if you see any cars."

He moved to the other side of the room where the windows looked out over the lane coming into the farm. He picked up a pair of binoculars from the table.

"It's a Wildlife and Fisheries truck sitting by my mailbox," he said, his voice bouncing off the windowpane.

"How do you know all this?" she asked into the phone. "You do. But how do you know they discovered us? ...The fliers?" She cupped her hand over the mouthpiece again. The Baron was trying to overhear the conversation.

"Baron, how did you get the fliers to our bidders?"

He put the binoculars down. "Vince delivered them, Liebchen. Nobody could intercept them. We're safe."

"It's impossible. All the bidders are reliable. We sent them privately!"

Wednesday, May 21, 1958, 11:00 a.m.
Grinnell Mill Woods

Florence and Jesse left the Stevenson covered bridge and rode over a half hour until they reached the bridge over the Little Miami River, next to the Grinnell Mill.

"How do we know they were here?" Jesse asked. A couple cars drove by them as they scoured the riverbank.

"We have to think like a fox," said Florence, and she lifted her bike over the railing and laid it on the ground. "Come on."

Jesse followed her and then saw what had gotten her attention. A simple sheet of paper on the end of a twig. Both knew that Sally had been there. Florence laid her bike down and ran to the twig.

"I believe this is for you," she said handing him the sketch page without even looking at it. He smiled as he unfolded it.

"Look at this."

"Wow. How does she do this? They are so cute." The sketch was of a mother and baby fox.

"Once she gets it in her head, she can sketch them a hundred times."

"You two are so special."

"What do you mean?" Jesse asked, looking at Florence now but still holding the sketch.

"In love, and all that."

Jesse looked startled. "We're just friends! We're all just friends."

"Jesse, if you tell Sally that you are just friends, you better watch out what she does. She told us about when you guys first met. You know, clover bracelets."

"We were eight years old."

"Well, she remembers it all. Your vows and everything."

Jesse stood there in deep thought. "She told you?"

Suddenly, Florence's body language changed drastically. "Jesse, we need to be careful."

"What?" He started to turn around, but Florence caught him by the shoulder.

"Don't look. One of those guys we saw at the museum is looking at us through the window." Florence suddenly looked afraid. She turned back toward her bike. Jesse followed suit.

At that moment Vince Aldridge pulled his Suburban to the other side of the bridge railing, got out, reached over the railing and, one by one grabbed the two bicycles and stowed them in the back of the vehicle. "Get in," he shouted at Florence and Jesse. He opened the passenger door.

"Do as he says," said the Baron, who walked from around the bush holding a pistol. "Look at what your meddling has done!" Florence was shaking now. Jesse tried to remain calm.

"Come on children," said Fraulein Schmidt, who followed the Baron. "You have no choice."

"We didn't do anything. We're sketching animals," Florence said bravely.

"Well, show us," said Vince, looking up and down the road.

"Here," said Jesse. "Foxes!"

Fraulein Schmidt took the sketch sheet from Jesse. "Nice. Very nice."

"Now, let us go. We didn't do anything. I'm sorry we were on your property," said Jesse.

"Sorry, kids. We saw you messing with my beaver trap. You probably let my eagles loose, too," said Vince.

"Vince, take them to the Mill." said Fraulein Schmidt. "We'll deal with them there."

"I'll put them downstairs where the animals are. Max can tie them to the chairs," said Vince.

Florence and Jesse looked at each other. Jesse stepped back but the woman grabbed Florence's arm and he relented.

CHAPTER 20

Wednesday, May 21, 1958, 11:00 a.m.
Trailside Museum

Montana and the others parked their bikes in the racks just outside the museum. Sally grabbed her sketch book and took it directly to Mr. MacCarthy.

"Will this work, Mr. MacCarthy?" Just then, Janice walked into the museum.

"Look, Janice. What do you think?"

"It's beautiful." She studied it closely. "They look so real. What size do you want it?"

"Well, we need it to fill three quarters of the back cover and your photo will fill three quarters of the front. I'll work on the titles and descriptions."

Janice went into the darkroom to finish the project holding the camera and Sally's sketch.

"Where's Jesse and Florence?" asked Mrs. MacCarthy. I've got sandwiches for you if you're hungry."

"You bet," said William.

"They should be here soon. They were a couple hours behind us and that's about how long we were hunting down the foxes," said Montana.

"And dodging raindrops," said Dale.

"Oh, that reminds me. Jesse called. You all passed."

They looked at each other and smiled. Especially Dale, who seemed to have a weight lifted off his shoulders. Philmont was a possibility for his summer.

Wednesday, May 21, 1958, 11:10 a.m.
Grinnell Mill Apartment

Vince and Max tied the hands of Jesse and Florence onto the chairs with the rope they used to climb the tree and steal the two eagles. Jesse could tell the chairs were old. One nearly fell apart as he scooted to get closer to Florence, who had silent tears running down her cheeks.

"Look." He nodded toward a plank table. Something moved and they could see the beaver munching on small twigs and leaves. Then they heard the steps.

"How are our intruders," said the Baron in his thick German accent.

"They are being very quiet," said Max.

"What are you doing here?" asked the Baron.

"We were meeting our friends. We are making a pamphlet of animals. That's all. The fox was our last drawing. They're going to wonder where we are. They're expecting us at the museum," said Jesse.

"They'll be looking for us," Florence added.

"We'll let you go. But not right now," said the Baron.

"I found all the buyers but the Chinese one," said Fraulein Schmidt.

"Do you think he's the one that leaked our plans to the authorities?" asked the Baron.

"If so, I'm surprised. I figured he would have the high bid. He wants those eagles."

"What did that guy on the phone offer?"

"$3,000 apiece. $200 each for the falcons."

Florence and Jesse looked at each other, surprised. That's when Jesse noticed the second cage on the table, obscured from their view by the cage with Mr. Beaver in it.

"Come upstairs, Liebchen, let's get everything ready for the auction."

"I thought you were selling them to the local guy," said the Baron.

"Not as long as there is someone who will pay more."

"Max, keep an eye on the kids. I don't trust them," said Vince, and the three went upstairs.

Jesse and Florence sat, tied to the chairs, in a room that smelled like dust and wet fur.

"Do you think they will let us go?" said Florence.

"I'm not sure they can."

Wednesday, May 21, 1958, 11:30 a.m.
Trailside Museum

"Where's the other roll of film, Dale?" asked Janice as she came out of the dark room.

"In the camera bag."

"Nope," she said. "It has the pictures we took at the park."

"The geese?" asked Sally.

Dale had that look you get when you know you had something, it's missing now, and you start retracing every single thing you did in the near past, hour by hour, minute by minute. "I slipped after we photographed the fox. It has to be there."

"Well, before going to all that trouble, double check all the pockets and cases and bicycle baskets. Do you remember where you slipped?" said Mr. MacCarthy.

"I think so."

They finally decided that they'd have to go back down to the Mill. They finished their sandwiches and hopped on their bikes. "All for one, one for all," said William as they pedaled down Correy Street to the Mill.

"Shouldn't we run into Florence and Jesse?" asked Dale.

"I hope so. They should be back by now," said Montana, slightly worried.

Dale led them past the Mill, and they moved their bikes over the railing and hid them behind the bush.

"They were here!" said Sally. "I left a sketch for Jesse. Look. It's gone."

"We must have passed them somehow."

"That means they're okay. Let's find the film." Dale led them up the riverbank to the spot where he had slipped. "Here. Help me look here."

They searched the entire riverbank but found no film. "It should be here. It's yellow."

"Hmm. Jesse found the love note Sally left. Maybe he found the film canister," said Montana.

"It wasn't a love note," Sally said, a little too quickly. "But you're right."

"It's a yellow canister," said Dale.

She continued staring at the tracks near where Dale had slipped. Then she bent over.

"Did you say yellow? Wait here."

She carefully took off her shoes and waded out into the river. After a few steps, she stepped closer to the riverbank and grabbed up a rodent from the grassy bank. "Here he is. I found the robber." She held up a rat with a long tail and the film canister firmly clenched in his teeth. He went to bite Montana, letting loose the canister, Montana caught it with her one hand, and let go of the rat with her other and the rodent swam back to the bank and quickly into his den on the riverbank.

Montana walked back up as if nothing spectacular had just happened and pitched the film to Dale. He put it in his pocket.

"How did you know that?" Dale reached down to help her back up the riverbank.

"Fresh tracks. Have you heard of a pack rat? He must have pushed on it because it left an impression in the mud. No telling what he has in his den."

Something caught Montana's eye. She stepped toward the path, never letting go of Dale, and pulled him behind an oak.

"What are you kids doing here?" Vince asked.

"Shh," Montana whispered. "He can't see us."

"Nothing," said William.

"Sketching animals," said Sally.

"Hmm. How many kids does it take to sketch animals?" Vince now had his pistol aimed at Sally. "You kids come with me. We'll put you with the other two."

William and Sally started walking toward the mill, Vince just a step behind them.

"Wait. We didn't do anything," said William.

"What do we do? He's got a gun," whispered Dale to Montana.

"Wait. Let's think. He said something about the other two. That means he has Jesse and Florence in the mill," said Montana.

"We have to get close to the mill." She peeked around the tree. "See that side of the mill?"

"Yeah. The side with no windows."

"No windows. Right! Follow me."

She and Dale walked upriver until the trees completely hid their movements and then turned back toward the mill. They used the trees as cover and one by one, got within fifty feet of the building.

"Let's go!" she said and ran to the mill and then crept to the rear where the damaged water wheel connected to the building. The stream that had fed the wheel nearly a century before was now a dry bed of stone and weeds.

Dale peeked through the opening where the drive shaft of the wheel penetrated the stone wall.

"Shh," he said when he returned to Montana. "They have Jesse and Florence. They're tying up Sally and William."

"We need to get help. I wish we knew what was going on there. Did you hear anything?"

"No. Nobody was saying anything. Wait here."

"No. I'm coming with you." As they went back to the rear of the mill, Dale picked up a flat stone from the dry stream bed.

They carefully positioned themselves in the water wheel. Dale got very close to the rusty drive shaft and tapped a couple times on it. He watched, hoping that he would get a reaction.

I SEE YOU, DALE, he tapped in Morse code and carefully watched. He thought he saw Jesse.

NOD. He tapped. Immediately, he saw Jesse smile and nod.

"He heard it," he whispered.

Wednesday, May 21, 1958, 12:00 p.m.
Grinnell Mill Apartment

"William and Sally, they let us go to the bathroom. Do you have to go?" Jesse said while Max and Vince were tying Sally and William.

William and Sally looked puzzled but once they looked at Jesse and the 'go along with this' look that Jesse gave, Sally said, "Please. I really have to go. Please."

Vince rolled his eyes, annoyed. "You finish tying that guy. I'll take her upstairs. You first, pretty girl." He followed her up the narrow stairs.

"Hey Max, do you know Morse code?" asked Jesse.

"I heard of that." He just finished tying William to his chair.

"M A X. He said the dits and dahs loud enough hoping that Dale would pick up the signal. D I D Y O U R E A D?"

"I got the dit dit. What was the rest?" Max said.

Jesse hesitated, and then he heard the taps for Y E S and G O O D which established the line of communication between him and Dale.

Dale tapped on the metal drive shaft.

W E N E E D T O K N O W W H A T I S G O I N G O N.

"Max, are they going to sell these eagles?" Jesse asked very loudly.

"What do you care?"

G O O D was tapped out by Dale.

"Are you going to let us go, Max? We didn't do anything."

"Don't you kids worry none. We'll let you go when we get rid of the birds."

The beaver was working on the limb and by now all the bark was ripped off.

"He looks like Paddles," Jesse whispered to Florence.

She just stared ahead, obviously frightened. She kept fidgeting with her ropes.

Jesse looked over to William with a desperate face. "Doesn't that beaver look like Paddles?" he said with emphasis on 'beaver' and 'Paddles.'

Florence looked at William. William nodded toward the beaver. Florence looked at the beaver, smiled, then nodded to Jesse.

Just then, Sally came down the steps.

"Okay, who else?" said Vince as he led Sally to her chair. She stumbled and fell on William.

"Go to the bathroom," she whispered.

Max started tying her arms to the back of the chair.

"I do. Please," said William.

As Vince and William cleared the stairs Max stood up from tying Sally's arms.

"Max, I'm worried about the eagles," came a small voice from the table.

Florence looked at Jesse and Sally and then got this amazed look on her face. Jesse and Sally got the same look.

"Who said that?" asked Max.

He looked around and all eyes were on the beaver, now sitting upright in its cage.

"They need to eat and I'm out of bark. I need more bark."

Max looked at the kids again and then back at the table. He leaned over the cage.

"What did you say, little fellow," he whispered so low the kids could not hear him.

CHAPTER 21

Wednesday, May 21, 1958, 12:10 p.m.
Grinnell Mill Apartment

Once William was in the bathroom, he looked everywhere trying to find the reason Sally thought he should go to the bathroom. *Why does she want me in this room?*

"I swear that sound came from the cage," came this voice from under the floor. He realized he was just above the room where part of the Wesley Club was being held hostage. It wasn't so much directly above but he could hear the voices. He studied the floor and noticed pieces of toilet paper covering the seams where the boards came together. He pulled out his pen knife and fiddled with the boards. They were just lying in place, not nailed to the joists. He carefully lifted one board and could see directly below. He could hear the kids and Max but could not see them. He leaned down closer and realized it was a separate room.

One by one, he lifted enough boards to create an opening large enough for him to drop through to the lower level.

Wednesday, May 21, 1958, 12:20 p.m.
Grinnell Mill Cellar

"It came from the cage, alright," said Jesse.

Max turned from the table and stared at the three teenagers tied to their chair. Florence looked him straight in the eye.

"I need bark." Florence lips did not move, and the voice definitely came from the cage. Max's eyes got big, and he turned back to the cage. "And the eagles are hungry."

He looked back at the kids, now just as wide-eyed and surprised that a beaver could be talking to a Canadian kidnapper.

"These kids are scared, look at them," said the beaver.

Now Max stepped back toward the stairs.

"Maybe it was one of the eagles," said Florence.

"Eagles can't talk. Only crows and parrots can talk," said Max.

"Then it has to be the beaver," said Sally.

He came back to the table. His stare was so intense, the beaver stared back, like it knew what the kids were up to. Once the beaver tilted its head, "You're gonna get caught Max. And go to prison. You know that." Max turned and clamored up the stairs.

"Vince. Come here. You've got to see this," he yelled.

While he was upstairs looking for Vince, William surprised the kids when he came into the room and loosened the ropes, just enough that they could wiggle out at any time. "That bathroom has a hole in it! Stay here while I check out the rest of the building," he said.

"I thought so," said Sally.

"Dale and Montana are outside," said Jesse.

"They better hide because they'll be looking for me pretty quick," said William.

Wednesday, May 21, 1958, 12:25 p.m.
Grinnell Mill Woods

"You heard them. Let's go back to the woods," said Montana. They both looked around the corner and lit off to a large clump of bushes at the edge of the wooded section.

"What do we do now?" said Dale.

"We have to get them out of that building."

"Look." Dale pointed at a car pulling up to the front of the mill. Two men got out, one carrying a brown briefcase, the other with dark glasses.

"Is there any other way out of the building?"

"Let's look around."

CHAPTER 22

Wednesday, May 21, 1958, 12:30 p.m.
Grinnell Mill Apartment

"Beavers don't talk, you idiot," said Vince as he and Max descended the stairs.

"Where's William? What did you do with him?" said Sally once they both were in the room.

"He's still in the loo," said Vince. "Show me," he said to Max.

"Over here. Watch." Both men stood over the beaver cage. Florence looked at Jesse. He shook his head ever so slightly.

Silence.

"Well?" Vince said as they stood there.

"Are you still hungry, little guy?" Max said to the beaver, who just sat there.

"You want some bark, huh, little buddy?" Vince stood up and looked around the room, one by one focusing on each of the kids tied to their chairs. "I swear. He asked for more bark."

"Beavers don't talk, you idiot! Go upstairs and bring that kid downstairs. We've got people showing up. We're doing the hawks first, then we'll want the eagles."

"He talked! I swear. You never believe me," said Max, still standing by the beaver cage.

"Get the kid." Vince went upstairs and reluctantly, Max followed him.

In moments, Max was back with William, to everyone's surprise. Max tied him to the chair and then went over to the beaver cage.

"They wouldn't believe you, would they?" said Mr. Beaver.

Max got closer to the cage. "Did you hear the beaver talk to me?"

"I heard someone," said Florence.

"You know this place is haunted don't you?" asked William.

Max looked around the room, suddenly aware of the shadows and cobwebs.

Wednesday, May 21, 1958, 12:40 p.m.
Grinnell Mill Apartment

"Ah. Everyone is here but one, but we can't wait," said the Baron. "We'll start the bidding with these four falcons. Let's start at $200 each."

Five bidders stood around the table with falcon cages. All men, some finely dressed, and one in particular, wore old time clothes like you'd see in a 1920's movie. He seemed to have this permanent smile on his face.

"I'll give $250 for one falcon."

"$300 each for all four."

"$325 each."

"$400!"

"I have $400 each for all four. Do I hear $500?"

"$400. Going once. Going twice. Sold to the man in the beret. You have made a fine deal." The man pulled out a large money bag from inside his coat and counted out sixteen one-hundred dollar bills.

"Vince, bring up those eagles," said the Baron.

Vince went down the stairs and found Max, still staring at the beaver.

"Vince, this place is haunted," he said, eyes on the beaver, waiting for its next words.

"Max. What is wrong with you? Help me with the eagles."

"That beaver told me to feed the eagles before we sold them, or they will die. We can't let them die, Vince."

"Have you been taking those pills, Max. You're going loony."

"Seriously, Vince, you have to believe the beaver."

Vince glared at him. "Here. Now carry this one upstairs. I'll bring the other one." Vince looked around the room to be sure the kids were still tied up in their appointed chairs, which formed a semi-circle around the table now holding only the cage with the beaver. They all had a view of the stairwell going upstairs.

"It won't be long, kids. We're just about finished."

As they went upstairs, there was a knock at the door.

"I know how to get us out of here," said William once Vince and Max cleared the stairs. Florence and Sally sighed in relief.

Wednesday, May 21, 1958, 1:00 p.m.
Grinnell Mill Cellar

Fraulein Schmidt answered the door and welcomed in the man.

"Your invitation, please."

"I phoned you earlier. My invitation was by phone. You remember."

"Ah, Mr. Gregory. You are the attorney."

"Please. I'm here for a client who cannot attend. It must be discreet," he whispered.

"Ah, Mr. Wong. He is the only person not present," she whispered.

He pulled out a handkerchief and wiped his brow, now perspiring. "Yes. Now, can we proceed."

Once he entered the room, he was overwhelmed by sight of the two American Bald Eagles perched beside each other, tethered to the post.

"They are beautiful," he said.

"You have cash?" asked the Baron.

Mr. Gregory set down his briefcase and opened it, displaying packs of $20 and $50 bills. "Can we begin?" he asked.

As the Baron started the bidding, there was another knock at the door. Vince answered it.

"My name is Mr. Wong. I believe you are expecting me. Good afternoon, Fraulein Schmidt."

CHAPTER 23

Wednesday, May 21, 1958, 1:05 p.m.
Grinnell Mill Apartment

The kids gasped as Vince led Mr. Gregory down the stairs at gunpoint.

"What are you doing here? Didn't you know we had this under control?" he said.

"We were caught looking for the fox. We were finishing the pamphlet," said William.

"Kinda," said Sally. "It's a real long story."

"Why are you here? What happened?" asked Florence.

"It's okay. We'll be fine," he said as Vince tied his arms to the last chair in the room.

"So, you all know each other. This is interesting. The Baron will be very interested in this. I wouldn't plan on getting out of here any time soon," said Vince.

Wednesday, May 21, 1958, 1:10 p.m.
Outside Grinnell Mill Apartment

Dale and Montana circled the building and found a small door that led to the lower level. It wouldn't open, but they were sure it was latched from the inside. When they got completely around, they crouched by the mill wheel. Dale took up his position as observer.

"They have Mr. Gregory. They just tied him to the chair," said Dale.

"We have to do something. Let me think. What are they talking about?" asked Montana.

"Before Mr. Gregory got there, they were talking about the place being haunted. They had Max convinced the Mill has ghosts." Then Dale paused a moment. "Wait, the other guy went back upstairs."

"Is Max still there?"

"Yes. He's staring at the cage with the beaver in it."

"Let's give them their ghosts. Tell Jesse ghosts are coming."

Without hesitation Dale tapped G H O S T S A R E C O M I N G.

Jesse looked at the other kids, sighed deeply, then said to Max, "We've seen ghosts, Max. Have you ever seen a ghost?"

"There's no such thing."

Suddenly there was a huge clank coming from the drive shaft of the mill wheel.

"I think there is. Did you hear that?"

Bang.

The sound was much louder.

"I believe in ghosts," said the beaver.

"No. No. Please. No." Max was now focused on the cage.

Sally motioned for Florence to continue.

"Have you ever seen a ... beaver ghost?" said the beaver.

Clank. Clank. Clank.

The sound reverberated through the building. Jesse, suddenly yelled, "Ghost! Help! Ghosts!" And with his outburst, the others joined in, including Max, who was the first to reach the stairs and head up them.

Sally loosened her rope and, now out of sight of Max, slipped behind Mr. Gregory and untied his rope. Jesse untied William.

"This way," said William once he was untied. He led everyone to another room on the lower level and a second set of stairs that went back up into the first level. When they reached a door that led to the auction room, Mr. Gregory grabbed William's arm.

"Wait," said Mr. Gregory. "Tell me what you see, William."

William peeked into the room. "Three men, Vince is holding onto Max. He's trying to go outside. The Schmidt woman is trying to settle down the eagles. The Baron is opening the front door."

"Where's Vince now?" Mr. Gregory whispered to William.

"He's behind the door and has his gun pulled."

"Who's at the door?"

"No one. Wait. It's Montana. She's got weeds and stuff all over her. She's soaking wet. She's in trouble."

Wednesday, May 21, 1958, 1:20 p.m.
Grinnell Mill Apartment

The entire room was focused on the tall red-haired teenager, soaking wet with weeds and vines hanging from her body. Her face was covered with dripping mud. She walked like the zombies do in the movies and each person in the room made way for each step she took.

Vince moved into her path from the back of the door, gun drawn, and just as he reached for her, Montana reached into her shirt and pulled out a snake. Vince took a step back and she flipped the snake onto him in such a way that it clung to his neck. He immediately dropped his gun and like a professional hockey player Montana kicked it through the throng of bidders, so it landed immediately in front of William, who picked it up and handed it to Mr. Gregory.

The Baron stepped toward her, and this time she pulled two snakes from her shirt and flung them in his face. One fell onto his hand and the other slipped down the neck of his shirt.

"Screech. Screeeech." Montana shrieked. Immediately the eagles and the hawks took flight in the barn-like room, one grabbing up Vince's toupee in its talons and dropping it where two snakes were seeking refuge on the floor. The female eagle clung onto Fraulein Schmidt's beehive hairdo in such a way that it was face to face with her and constantly flapping its wings. The German woman fought with a fury, but her punches landed on her own head instead of the angry eagle.

Bidders began to scatter but Montana opened her shirt completely, dumping at least a dozen water snakes on the floor in front of them and the sight repelled them back toward Mr. Gregory, who, gun in hand, was working his way toward Montana.

Bang! The gun fired into the air and in an instant quiet filled the room and just as quickly, the bidders were surrounded by Fishery and Wildlife agents with rifles ready.

"Those are my eagles, and these are my snakes," Montana announced to everyone present, including the Wildlife agents. Though she was dressed like a swamp monster, her words were clear and brave. "I have to take them home." The entire Wesley Club gathered around her.

"I have to call Grandpa. We have to get the eggs back in the nest," said the erstwhile zombie.

"That's handled, Montana," came a familiar voice. "Mr. Atwell is on his way to the museum. You guys go ahead. Call me here when you want the eagles loosed." David handed her a piece of paper with the phone number of the apartment on it. The Wesley Club retrieved their bikes and sped to the Glen.

CHAPTER 24

Wednesday, May 21, 1958, 2:15 p.m.
Trailside Museum

Montana was the first to arrive at the Trailside Museum, and as the rest of the Wesley Club pedaled in, Mr. Atwell pulled into the driveway.

"We have to hurry," he said. "One of the eggs is hatching as we speak."

Mrs. MacCarthy was waiting with Montana's jacket which she traded for the slip of paper with the apartment phone number. Mr. Atwell gingerly placed an egg in each jacket pocket and, barefoot, Montana carefully ran down the 100 steps to the huge oak tree, the rest of the Wesley Club close behind.

"Leg up," she said.

William cupped his hand like a stirrup and in one motion lifted her up six feet. Moments later she was settled by the nest.

"Call David, Grandma!" she yelled from the nest.

After a very long two minutes, there was a screech from the sky as Montana carefully placed two active eggs precisely where they had been laid a month earlier. The male was first to land. He carefully inspected the nest.

Montana was worried as minutes flew by with the female eagle still missing.

"Grandpa. Where's the other eagle?" Montana whispered down the tree. The tree, by now, was surrounded by the Wesley Club, hikers and town residents who had become apprised of the day's events.

Screech. The male eagle alarmed Montana, causing her to scoot back on the limb, just as the second eagle landed, with a healthy bluegill in her mouth. Mrs. Eagle prepared the fish for her and her mate.

"Thank you, God."

Montana slowly scooted down the tree into the arms of her closest friends, the Wesley Club. There was applause from the gathering. Handshakes and hugs from everyone and when it was finally just the Wesley Club, under the tree, Montana MacCarthy held tight to her grandpa and started sobbing.

"I have to get those snakes back in the water, Grandpa."

"We got that," said David. "Kids, you just busted the biggest poaching ring this side of the Mississippi. They're all going to jail."

"Really?"

"Poor Max," said Florence. They all laughed. As the next few minutes progressed one set of the Wesley Club would tell what was going on inside the Grinnell Mill while Montana and Dale would describe gathering up the water snakes.

"You asked for a ghost," Montana said, picking water crest and weeds out of her hair, and they all broke into laughter once again.

"We're not finished," said Janice. "Here, Montana. I've made sure the settings are right. All you do is click and advance." She showed Montana each button on the camera that created a picture. She laid the strap round Montana's neck like an Olympic medal. Montana looked puzzled.

"The eggs. Aren't they hatching?" Janice said.

Montana's eyes went wide. She studied the camera's buttons and then smiled.

"Leg up!" she said.

William responded, lifting the teenager high up to the first limb.

When she got back to the nest, the eagles were still feasting on the blue gill fish.

"Hi, guys. Mind if I watch?"

By now the birds had become accustomed to Montana.

"Montana!" yelled Mr. MacCarthy. She looked down.

"Sometimes it takes days for the birds to hatch. One egg will start first. You'll probably have to come down in between pictures for breaks."

She watched Mrs. Eagle stand up from the eggs and inspect them, using her beak to adjust their position. There was a hole on one egg a full inch across. Montana snapped a photo. *Click.* Mrs. Eagle glared at Montana for a moment and then snuggled back down on the eggs.

Mr. Eagle stood up and grabbed the bony leftovers from the fish with his talon and hopped to the edge of the nest and flew off.

Mrs. MacCarthy joined the circle of well wishers at the base of the oak.

"Montana's getting pictures of the fledglings," said Grandpa MacCarthy.

"Not with all that yucky mess all over her. Erin Montana MacCarthy! Get down here right now or you'll catch your death of cold!"

Montana was not ready to abandon the eggs.

"It's okay," said Mr. MacCarthy. "Get cleaned up. Then you can come back. Those eggs will take hours to hatch.

"C'mon Montana," said Sally.

"Leg up!" said Janice, and William hoisted Janice Pyle to the first oak limb. She studied the nest and the limbs leading to it and stopped on the limb just below Montana.

"Hand me the camera. I'll watch until you come back."

"I don't want to leave them," Montana said.

"Well, you already stink from those snakes. Go get cleaned up before David shows up. Take over when you come back."

Montana handed over the camera and climbed down the tree. Then Janice took her position in the tree.

One Hour Later

"Leg up!" said Montana, now wearing bib overalls and a Buckeye Lake t-shirt. Janice motioned her to hurry.

"I see feathers," Janice said when Montana reached the limb with the nest.

Mrs. Eagle stood up again and nudged the two eggs, and suddenly the beak of the first fledgling erupted through the hole in the shell and the protective membrane.

Click. Janice had just the right angle.

"There's a newspaper guy down there from the Springfield paper," said Montana. He wants a picture of the nest.

"Does he know what you guys went through?"

"Yeah. He said he talked to David at the police station."

Screech! Screech! Went Mrs. Eagle. A moment later Mr. Eagle hopped into the nest with a small mouse.

"Here's the camera. My butt hurts. I'll bring back fresh film," said Janice.

"Sally wants to come up here," said Montana.

"Okay. Let's see what we can do."

"Janice, can you come down? They're here to see the pictures," said Mr. MacCarthy.

"Mr. MacCarthy! We don't allow tree climbing in the Glen," said a woman wearing khaki shirt and bloused slacks.

"Well. This is special. This is for the pamphlet."

"I thought you were done!"

"A pair of eagles have slightly delayed our last photo."

The woman looked up into the tree.

"Two eagle eggs are hatching up there as we speak. We'll have pictures soon."

The woman aimed her binoculars up toward the nest.

Janice called for help and dropped down into the arms of Dale and William.

"Follow me, ma'am. I'll show you our pamphlet," said Janice.

One Hour Later

"Number one is out of the shell," Montana whispered down to the eagle watchers below the nest. She then, limb by limb, with the help of William, dropped to the floor of the forest. She handed the camera to Janice.

"I think I was making them nervous. I'll check on them in the morning."

"Who are those guys?" She was referring to three men standing halfway up the 100 steps and talking with Jesse, Janice, and Dale.

"Let's go talk to them," said her grandpa.

Wednesday, May 28, 1958, 2:15 p.m.
Shawnee Park

"I got it!" Jesse Hall pulled his bike to the bike rack, lifted his sister off the handle bars and hurried to the picnic table where the rest of the Wesley Club was seated.

"They just came into the drug store." He laid out a copy of *Field and Stream* magazine on the table.

"Your picture is everywhere! Montana, you're famous!"

"Miss Montana MacCarthy, now that you have single handedly nabbed the Canadian poachers, with your trained snakes, and became famous, how do you feel?" Sally asked, holding her sketching pencil like a microphone.

"Well, they shouldn't have messed with my eagles."

"What will you do now that you're famous?"

"Just what I do best. Protect my Forest," and she turned her head so that the wind caught her red hair and blew it like a flag.

Hoot. Hoot. The Saw Whet owl replied from a nearby buckeye tree.

The End

DISCUSSION QUESTIONS

1. The story opens with two poachers trying to steal an American Bald Eagle from a forest even though it was against the law. Why were they doing that?
2. In Chapter 2, Montana was able to walk up to a family of deer and get very close. Where did she get the skill to do that?
3. Why was Montana living alone with her grandmother and grandfather?
4. The Wesley club said grace over their lunch at school. How did the other school kids respond to that?
5. What caused the Wesley Club to be captured by the poachers?
6. Montana did some daring things in the story, like stand in a pond to catch a bat in her hand, get close to skunks, and gather up water snakes, to name a few. Were those all brave things she did? What made her brave?

7. The Wesley Club is full of special kids with unique abilities. What is something you are really gifted at?

8. Why did the Baron and Vince threaten the kids with guns?

9. Montana told David that God wanted her to protect the animals. How do you think she knew that?

REVIEWS – WESLEY CLUB ADVENTURE SERIES

Amazon Reviewer: This book was so good that I read it one

day. I loved all the characters and the story line was so captivating. Florence had a misfortune happen to her parents. But with the support of family and friends, she was able to maneuver through the ups and downs. I'm looking forward to reading this whole series.

Amazon Reviewer: At almost 60 years old, I loved the Jesse series and read *Florence's Journey* in one day. You become attached to the characters and feel their fears, sadness and triumph. I hope that the Florence series continues.

I loved this book 2 in this authors new series A Wesley Club Adventure. It was about a girl who is protecting the animals in the forest. Her love for animals is so endearing and special. This author captures the beauty and authenticity in children in all the books he writes. His books are so wonderful for kids because they are clean and simple but have a message in each one that is educational. I highly recommend reading these books for young and old and in between.

—L Martin

Professional Reviewer: *Florence's Journey: Proving Something* is the first book in the Wesley Club series for young readers and follows nine-year-old Florence Abigail Williams, who is, as the story opens convinced that her mother's reference to a 'surprise' means many possibilities of an improvement to their home and lives.

Surprise! It involves a journey that, in 1955 Ohio, is no light undertaking when Florence's parents are accused of a crime and arrested, leaving Florence with too many questions and an uncertain future.

Florence's diary entries describing her experience juxtapose with third person observations of trials, errors, and foster homes that teach Florence about different worlds and lives.

As her parents learn how to parent from a distance and maintain contact with Florence, the child embarks on a new life under vastly revised conditions, learning to participate in the community church and life in a very different way.

It doesn't help their case that her parents don't recall where they were or what happened, so Florence becomes involved in an investigation that holds some surprising twists and turns.

It's unusual to see a pre-teen read where the young protagonist is unwittingly pulled into an adult world of legal and criminal processes while simultaneously navigating her own understanding of strange circumstances. The intrigue added by Florence's own perception of those who arrested her parents introduces another layer of possibility to the mystery that young people won't see coming (and neither will adults).

As time goes by, Florence's ability to adapt to new circumstances and participate in rebuilding not just her life, but those of her parents, creates a moving and engrossing story that flavors its backdrop of 1950s Ohio with social observations and spiritual reflection.

The mystery, character development, and spiritual growth dovetail nicely with scenes that profile both the times and the proactive determination of a young girl charged with getting her family back together against all odds and impossible circumstances.

Libraries and readers looking for realistic stories of trials, difficult choices, and a savvy, concerned child who might be the only one able to help her parents resolve their own unexpected struggles will find *Florence's Journey: Proving Something* an astute story of courage, conviction, and spiritual growth. It ideally will attract a wide audience. This is the first book of the Wesley Club Adventure series.

—D. Donovan – Midwest Book Review

Professional Review: I must say, this is a very enjoyable mystery novel for 9 – 12-year-olds. The writer, Victor Hess, works hard to offer his readers a host of memorable, young characters and a tantalizing mystery for them to solve. So, what's it about? Well, in a nutshell, a young girl named Florence is left to defend for herself when her parents are accused of a robbery. Set in the 1950s, the story follows Florence as she's moved from house to house, until she ends up living with her aunt and meeting the Wesley Club.

This is a skillfully plotted novel written by an author who knows how to keep things simple – but not too simple. The focus is kept on Florence and how her character develops when she's thrown in the deep end of life. In many ways, it's as much a coming-of-age story as it is a mystery, and it's this mix that is its biggest strength.

So, what needs work? To be honest, not a lot. The start's a bit low, and there's the odd clumsy sentence, but nothing big; nothing that pulls away from the compelling plot. In fact, the only part of the book I didn't like was the title; I just felt it lacked oomph and might put a lot of young readers off.

All in all, I'm very happy to recommend this book to 9 – 12-year-olds looking for a character led story with a strong, charismatic protagonist. I think they'll enjoy getting to know Florence and following her on her 'journey'. I also think the mystery of her parents' crime and how the Wesley Club help her to find answers is compelling. I understand this is the first book in the set; if so, then I very much look forward to reading the rest and seeing what the Wesley Club get up to next!

—A 'Wishing Shelf' Book Review

Montana's Mission is a captivating story with a poignant and increasingly relevant message about wildlife conservation. Although aimed at young readers, I think adults will find this sleuth mystery adventure tale engrossing. Author Victor Hess doesn't miss a beat, drawing the reader's attention from the get-go and holding it until the end with some well-placed twists and turns of the plot and a vibrant cast of characters. Hess's writing exudes a sense of realism that makes the stakes feel all the higher, and you find yourself constantly on the edge of your seat, wondering what's coming next.

Montana and her friends display a believable dynamic between them that you see among young teenagers in real life. As an animal lover and a reader of mystery adventure novels, I thoroughly enjoyed this book. I think kids and young adults will have a blast with this one.

—Readers' Favorite Five Star Review

BIO

Victor Hess' fifth book, *Montana's Mission: Protecting the Forest*, is the second work in his Wesley Club Mystery Adventure series. His fiction is based on his experiences as a young boy in the 50's and 60's in the Midwest. He writes literature based on Christian values and how very young people have gifts to help them succeed in overwhelming conditions. His writing has earned recognition in the William Faulkner – William Wisdom Creative Writing competition in New Orleans for multiple years. His first book, Jesse Sings was a finalist in the 2018 Best American Books competition. His books have been featured at the Ohioana Book Festival where he served on the Historical Fiction Panel, Louisiana Book Festival, and the Mississippi Book Festival. He served in the military, taught Sunday School and Bible Study for decades, and finally settled back in his Ohio hometown after retiring from a business career. There, he continues writing full-time.

OTHER BOOKS BY VICTOR HESS

SEARCHING FOR FAMILY SERIES REVIEWS FROM READERS

"Hess is masterful at capturing the naivete and innocence of a young boy in difficult circumstances."

"Love, Love, Love, this book."

"I was captivated by Jesse's story, and his struggle to find normalcy in a dysfunctional world. His character is believable and presents a poignant viewpoint in a voice that makes you feel as if you're viewing the world through a young boys eyes."

"A deeply moving coming-of-age novel."

".. Dickensian bleak, but his spirit is indomitable."

"I decided to get this book because my son's name is Jesse. I'm glad I did. It was well written and all of my children enjoyed reading it and it kept their attention."

"Much like To Kill a Mockingbird, we see the story through a child's eyes. Set in Ohio during the simpler times of the 1950's, we see how Jesse heroically tries to live a normal life."

"This is the best coming-of-age book I've read to date."

"Would recommend to any age group."

—Amazon Readers. All reviews are listed on Amazon.

ACKNOWLEDGMENTS

This book could not have been written without the amazing support of Facebook book club members, my newsletter fans, my family, and my unbiased friends.

Readers from two writing groups helped brighten up various chapters:

Ohio Chapter of American Christian Fiction Writers - Critique Group

Sages Monthly Writing Workshop

The following books were instrumental in helping me write this story:

The trapper's bible: the most complete guide to trapping and hunting tips ever, Edited by Eustace Hazard Livingston, Skyhorse Publishing, 2012

Two hundred years of Yellow Springs: a collection of articles first published in the Yellow Springs News for the 2003 bicentennial of Yellow Springs, Ohio, Yellow Springs News, Inc, 2005

Covered Wood Truss Bridges of Greene County, Ohio, James H. Shell, 1998

Ohio's Covered Bridges, Elma Lee Moore, Arcadia Publishing, 2010

The cover was created by Ardent Artist Books, Trisha Fuentes, and it's my fifth book cover by her. She is also responsible for the interior formatting.

The editing as done by Katie Costello.

THANK YOU

If you enjoyed *Montana's Mission* and would like to keep up with other stories about the Wesley Club Mysteries, by Victor Hess, join hundreds of other readers by signing up for my newsletter which gives you chances to win neat stuff. New subscribers are entered into a special monthly drawing which includes a signed copy of at least one of my books each month.

https://victorhess.com/newsletter

And don't worry, I do not share any of your information with anyone ever.

Made in the USA
Monee, IL
20 October 2026

66035301R00142

Sitzungsberichte der Heidelberger Akademie der Wissenschaften

Mathematisch-naturwissenschaftliche Klasse

Die Jahrgänge bis 1921 einschließlich erschienen im Verlag von Carl Winter, Universitätsbuchhandlung in Heidelberg, die Jahrgänge 1922—1933 im Verlag Walter de Gruyter & Co. in Berlin, die Jahrgänge 1934—1944 bei der Weiß'schen Universitätsbuchhandlung in Heidelberg. 1945, 1946 und 1947 sind keine Sitzungsberichte erschienen.

Ab Jahrgang 1948 erscheinen die „Sitzungsberichte" im Springer-Verlag.

Inhalt des Jahrgangs 1948:

1. P. Christian und R. Haas. Über ein Farbenphänomen. DM 1.50.
2. W. Blaschke. Zur Bewegungsgeometrie auf der Kugel. DM 1.—.
3. P. Uhlenhuth. Entwicklung und Ergebnisse der Chemotherapie. DM 2.—.
4. P. Christian. Die Willkürbewegung im Umgang mit beweglichen Mechanismen. DM 1.50.
5. W. Bothe. Der Streufehler bei der Ausmessung von Nebelkammerbahnen im Magnetfeld. DM 1.—.
6. W. Troll. Urbild und Ursache in der Biologie. DM 1.50.
7. H. Wendt. Die Jansen-Rayleighsche Näherung zur Berechnung von Unterschallströmungen. DM 2.40.
8. K. H. Schubert. Über die Entwicklung zulässiger Funktionen nach den Eigenfunktionen bei definiten, selbstadjungierten Eigenwertaufgaben. DM 1.80.
9. W. Schaaff. Biegung mit Erhaltung konjugierter Systeme. DM 1.80.
10. A. Seybold und H. Mehner. Über den Gehalt von Vitamin C in Pflanzen. DM 9.60.

Inhalt des Jahrgangs 1949:

1. H. Maass. Automorphe Funktionen und indefinite quadratische Formen. DM 3.60.
2. O. H. Erdmannsdörffer. Über Fasergranite und Böllsteiner Gneis. DM 1.20.
3. K. H. Schubert. Die eindeutige Zerlegbarkeit eines Knotens in Primknoten. DM 2.80.
4. K. Holldack. Grenzen der Herzauskultation. DM 4.20.
5. K. Freudenberg. Die Bildung ligninähnlicher Stoffe unter physiologischen Bedingungen. DM 1.—.
6. W. Troll und H. Weber. Morphologische und anatomische Studien an höheren Pflanzen. DM 7.80.
7. W. Doerr. Pathologische Anatomie der Glykolvergiftung und des Alloxandiabetes. MD 9.80.
8. W. Threlfall. Knotengruppe und Homologieinvarianten. DM 1.50.
9. F. Oehlkers. Mutationsauslösung durch Chemikalien. DM 3.80.
10. E. Sperner. Beziehungen zwischen geometrischer und algebraischer Anordnung. DM 3.—.
11. F. Heller. Ursus (Plionarctos) stehlini Kretzoi. DM 4.80.
12. W. Rauh. Klimatologie und Vegetationsverhältnisse der Athos-Halbinsel und der ostägäischen Inseln Lemnos, Evstratios, Mytiline und Chios. DM 10.50.
13. Y. Reenpää. Die Schwellenregeln in der Sinnesphysiologie und das psychophysische Problem. DM 1.60.